Nash

Breeding Facility, Volume 6

S L Davies

Published by S L Davies, 2022.

This is a work of fiction. Similarities to real people, places, or events are entirely coincidental.

NASH

First edition. September 12, 2022.

Copyright © 2022 S L Davies.

ISBN: 979-8215407400

Written by S L Davies.

Prologue

M addox
(17 Years old)

"What the hell is this?" my Papa roared as he burst through my bedroom door.

I looked up from where I was sitting at my desk working on my latest assignment for school.

"What?" I asked, not sure what I'd done this time.

"This," Papa roared again as he shook a piece of paper in front of my face. His eyes were bulging, and his face was red. I wondered if he was about to burst.

I shook my head. "Papa, I don't know what that is."

Papa slammed the paper down on the desk in front of me. I gasped when I glanced down and saw that it was an acceptance letter for trade school. I'd applied for the universities that Papa had insisted on, but I knew that my grades were never going to be good enough to be accepted. Not that I wanted to be a doctor or lawyer. I wanted to be a carpenter. I wanted to work with my hands. I loved to build things.

Papa said it was nothing more than a hobby, but to me, it was the reason I had sanity. Living in a house with an abusive father and mother that was so meek and broken that she couldn't find it in herself to stand up for her only child, was hell. I needed something that allowed me to hide away from the ranting lectures or worse the punches.

"Papa," I started. *But what could I say?* I'd deliberately gone against him. I knew when I applied that he would be furious if he found out. Naively I thought I might have been able to hide the letter from him. I should've known better. Nothing came into this house without my Papa's knowledge.

Papa folded his arms across his chest and glared at me. "What the hell is that Maddox? Why are you receiving an acceptance letter from a trade school?" he spat with disgust threaded through his voice.

I sucked in a deep breath. My heart was pounding hard against my ribs. My legs desperately wanted to get up and run. I was terrified of this man. He was an alpha and I was born as a mere omega. In my father's mind, I owed him. I was a disappointment. I owed him for what he had lost when my Mama's family turned their back on her and him. And it was all because of me.

"I want to be a carpenter," I mumbled, I couldn't lift my eyes to look at Papa's face. I knew that it would be filled with disgust. I felt myself wanting desperately to revert in age. Papa didn't know it. It was my best kept secret. The one that I made sure to keep hidden from everyone. But when life got too hard or the beatings were more than I could take, I would hold my stuffy that I'd had since I was a baby, and suck on the pacifier that I'd bought secretly.

Papa snorted and laughed, but there was no humor in that sound. It was absolute hatred.

"A carpenter? That's what you want to be is it?" he sneered.

I bit into my bottom lip and nodded my head.

"Well, isn't that lovely? I go to work every day and work my fingers to the bone to make sure we can have the money that your Mama was accustomed to. You lost that money for me, the way you paraded yourself in front of that man. Now you refuse to do as I expect and earn the money I request of you, to pay me back for what you took," Papa spat.

I flicked my eyes up to his and saw that the vein in his forehead was pulsing. I wondered if this might be my last day on earth. *Had I pushed him too far?* I just wasn't sure.

Papa shook his head and curled his top lip. "So, why haven't you received any other acceptance letters?"

"I. My grades. They aren't good enough to get into those courses Papa," I said quietly.

Papa hummed in his throat. "So, why spend all this money on the best schools if you can't even do well enough to be something?"

I frowned and sighed deeply. "Papa I can do something with my life. A carpenter is a great job. I can make a lot of money doing it."

Papa's lip curled further, and his hands curled into fists. He lifted one fist and slammed it into the desk in front of me, sending a crack through the center. "No son of mine will be some filthy tradie. I won't tolerate it. Our name is better than that. I raised you to be better than that. You drop this nonsensical idea and apply yourself. I've thrown enough money at you. I expect you to do better."

"Papa I can't do any better. I can't make the universities take me if they don't want me. What do you expect me to do?" I argued.

No sooner had the words left my mouth than I knew that I'd fucked up. No one was allowed to argue with Joseph Chan. No one. With a lunge that beguiled his age, Papa grabbed me by the front of my shirt and lifted me clean out of my seat. My eyes widened and my mouth opened and closed as I tried to find a way to de-escalate the situation.

"Get the fuck out of my house," he snarled in my face. His arms shook under the weight it took to control himself.

I nodded my head. Tears burned at the back of my eyes as I licked over my bottom lip.

"I will," I promised.

Papa dropped me unceremoniously onto the floor. Without a second thought, I turned to where I'd left my backpack and started to throw a handful of clean clothes into the bag, before running out of my bedroom.

Mama stood at the front door. Her hands over her mouth as she watched me with wide eyes. I hesitated slightly in front of her. I didn't know what I was waiting for. Maybe I was hoping that this would be the time she would finally stand up to Papa. But instead, she closed her eyes and turned her back.

With a sigh, I took off out the door and never looked back. I would be a carpenter; I would find a way. At least with trade school, it was cheaper. I didn't know where to go. I had no idea what to do. I was terrified and an omega out on the streets at night. That was never an ideal situation.

After running for what felt like hours I finally flopped down into the gutter and tucked my bag into my lap. Tears fell over my cheeks as the sobs I'd been holding back finally surfaced and fell from my lips. I was officially homeless. I knew that Papa meant what he said. I was not going to be allowed back. There was no calming down and talking things out. Once Papa made a decision that was it.

"Maddox?" A voice called from behind me. I turned to see my woodwork teacher coming down the driveway of the house I'd collapsed in front of.

"Sorry Mr. Beard, I'll go," I said as I stood.

Mr. Beard shook his head and walked towards me. "No son, it's alright. Why don't you come inside and talk to me? Something obviously has you very upset."

I looked up and down the street. I wasn't sure that this was the right decision. *But what other option did I have?* It was either keep walking on the street or trust this human. I mean he was my teacher. Surely, he couldn't be that bad.

Chapter One

M addox
(Present time)

As it turned out going into Mr. Beard's house was the best decision I ever made. He became more than a teacher to me, but a parent. He and his wife, Tom, and Margaret. I was made feel completely welcomed. I'd sat at their kitchen table and poured out my entire soul. I told them all about Papa's abuse and anger. They listened to everything I had to say. There was not an ounce of judgment in them.

Tom had given my Papa a phone call. My Papa had laughed at Tom and wished him good luck, but I was no longer their son. Papa didn't care what happened to me. My heart was destroyed. Tom and Margaret quickly became my parents. They celebrated my wins and sat with me on my heartbreaks.

And they even encouraged me to go to trade school. I became a carpenter at the top of the class. Tom and Margaret along with their adult children, Alexander and Allison all came to my graduation. They took photos of me and celebrated with me. It was a bitter-sweet day, but a day I would do over and over for the memories that it created. My portrait still sits proudly on their wall along with Alexander and Allison's photos.

They were the best thing to ever happen to me. They were my family. When I decided to set up my own business, Tom had helped me work through all the financial things I would need. He helped me to apply for the loan that I needed to buy my own workshop and machines. He had my back every step of the way.

The day my workshop was ready and open, Tom and Margaret were my very first customers. Margaret wanted a new bedroom suite. The look on their faces when they saw what I created them. Margaret had burst into tears. At first, I thought maybe she didn't like it, but she told me the tears were happy tears. As far as I'm aware they still have that same bedroom suite to this day.

Everyone that Tom and Margaret spoke to they told them about their son who was a carpenter. Soon, I had more work than I could even fathom. It was like a snowball effect. My work was seen by others and people started to want to hire me for all kinds of jobs, from building houses to creating baby cribs.

I was only operating for a year when I had to employ more staff. Something I had never imagined. But once again Tom was able to help me to learn everything I needed. All the things that my father should have done.

Instead, my Papa didn't make a peep. I never saw or heard from him or Mama again. For the first few years, that silence hurt. But with every year that passed with not hearing from them the easier it became. To the point that now I barely even think of them. I didn't care what happened to them.

If they came looking for me now, they would see a man who was incredibly successful and turned a hobby into a profitable business that had me living in a very expensive house and brand-new cars every year. I was everything my Papa had wanted, but I didn't do it the way he wanted.

I was sitting in the office going over the paperwork. I'd just received two new permits for houses that we were preparing to build over the next few months. It was going to be a good few months and I knew that my crew was going to be happy for the work.

The door to the workshop buzzed and I stood to go out to the reception area. I grinned when I saw Anghus, the president of the Devil's Advocates coming in through the door.

"Anghus, good to see you, man," I said with a broad smile.

"Good to see you too," he replied, sticking his hand out to shake mine. "I've come to ask if you've got room to do a build for the Devil's?"

"That depends on how fast you need the job done. I've got a couple of builds coming up, so my crews are going to be pretty booked out."

Anghus shook his head and waved his hand. "It won't be ready to start for a few months yet. I've got to get the sign-off from the council and the architect to finish drawing up the plans."

I nodded my head. I'd done a lot of work on the Devil's Advocates compounds. They did amazing work in Lalbert. They seemed to be growing by the day. They now had two compounds that operated, but I'd heard talk that they were planning to move over to the second and use the other compound to rent out for single omegas. The work they did with omegas was amazing.

'So, what are you thinking?" I asked.

"A school building. With this war coming, I want all the supernatural kids to be well versed in their powers," Anghus replied.

I frowned. I'd heard the murmurs of a war against Ettore, the Nephilim. But I wasn't sure if it was just conspiracy.

"The war is real?" I questioned.

Anghus nodded. "Yep. I wish it wasn't, but fuck man, Ettore is evil. I don't know all the details, but he is planning on raising up an army of demons."

My eyes widened and I gasped. "Demons?"

Anghus nodded again and scrubbed his hand down over his beard. "Yeah. I fucking hate it. But it's not something I think we can avoid. So, I want to arm the kids as best we can."

. "Yeah, I get that. Shit. Alright, well when you have the plans, bring them in. You know that I'll do it for you."

Anghus grinned and tapped his knuckles on the reception table that stood between us. "That's great. Thanks, man. I'll see you soon."

I smiled and lifted my hand in a wave as I watched the giant gargoyle turn and leave the workshop. I huffed out a breath and rubbed my hands up over my face. A damned war. Like this world needed anymore. And an army of demons. That was fucking terrifying.

Chapter Two

N^{ash}

"Alright guys listen up," Kade said as he came in through the door to the shifter room. We'd all been working hard finding the missing kids that were now considered cold cases. The more we looked at them the more we realized that many of the cases had Ettore written all over them.

"Scout and Kaki have got a hit on the missing girl April O'Neal. She was taken in 1997. April is a witch omega, taken on her way home from school when she was thirteen years old. Scout was able to track her down to a breeding facility, from our research we've discovered that they currently have five omegas in the house. It is in Winchester, so the next town over, but I want to send you guys, as you have experience with the breeding facility raids."

"What do we know about the facility?" Memphis asked.

"Other than the fact that there are five omegas, April being the eldest. The others we believe are possibly her children. They range from the age of five to fifteen. Until we get April back here, we won't know anything about other children that she produced. Scout was able to tell us that the fifteen-year-old appears to be pregnant."

"Is it an Ettore facility?" Bacchus questioned.

Kade shook his head. "No, but the owners are involved with Morpheus. So, although it isn't being run by Ettore, it is associated. The owners are Leanne and Rachel Meyer. Two sisters. Witches. There aren't any arrests on their records and from the research, Onyx Rebels did we were able to find out that Leanne and Rachel grew up in a cult of witches. Basically, they despise men and boys. They believe that women are the ruling gender and don't need men. I suspect that any boys that were born into the facility were either sent to fight with Morpheus or killed."

I winced at the very idea. I hated it. "When do we go in?"

Kade looked down at his watch. "We will leave in two hours. Scout and Kaki have eyes on the house. The place is currently warded; however, Merza has been able to see the wards, she will break them just before we enter. We don't want the women to have any idea what is about to descend on them."

"So, do you want us to go in shifted?" Coltrane asked.

Kade hummed in his throat and twisted his lips in thought. "Yeah, that might be a good idea. Let's have half of you shifted and the other half in human form. The house is covered by woods, so it will be easier to track the sisters if they manage to escape."

"Are we teaming up with anyone else?" Memphis asked.

Kade nodded his head. "The Onyx Rebels will be there, and I've organized a team of witches from Winchester to meet us there also. From what Scout has told us the wards aren't strong, so they don't expect that the witches are very powerful. However, I don't want to underestimate them, just in case."

We all nodded our heads as Kade pulled up a map of the property and started to plot where each of us would enter. I was one of the shifted members, along with Pax and Coltrane. While Memphis, Bacchus, and Raiden would go in as humans. From the Onyx Rebels, Scout and Nova would be shifted and keep eyes from the sky, Scout being a raven shifter and Nova an owl shifter.

Bandit and Butler two humans would enter with Memphis, Bacchus, and Raiden. While Merza and Kaki along with the witch team from Winchester would take control of the wards. I always felt a little uncertain whenever we did a raid. As much as we could plan our point of attack, not all bases were covered. There was always a chance that things could go wrong.

By the time we were ready to leave, everyone wore the same look we had whenever we did a raid. The look of unadulterated anger. We hated crimes against children. I despised it. The rest of the team were all fathers, they felt it even stronger than I did. But I was a Daddy. I still felt that anger.

The drive out to Winchester was done in silence. Merza had gone over earlier to meet with the witch unit and make sure the wards were as we suspected. We hadn't heard anything more from them, so could only assume that everything was going as planned.

We pulled up on the outskirts of the forest and climbed out of the vans. Merza and the witches were standing in the tree line waiting for us.

"The wards will be easy to break," Merza said. "I can sense the power of two witches inside, but they aren't strong."

Kade nodded his head. "Right, those who are shifting, get shifted and head through the forest towards the house. Merza and the witch team, circle the edge of the wards and start breaking them, as soon as you give the signal, me, Memphis, Bacchus, Raiden, and the witch team will go in with Bandit and Butler."

Everyone made a noise of affirmation. I stripped out of my clothes and focused on the shape of my alter. My bones, muscles, and tendons moved and started to click into place. I felt my large antlers start to grow from my head. The world around me became sharper, sounds were clearer. I looked around the forest and saw that Coltrane and Pax were shifted beside me.

"Alright, ready?" Coltrane asked through the link.

"Let's go," I replied.

"Yep, let's do this," Pax said.

We each headed into the forest quietly. To anyone walking through the woods, they might think it strange to see a rhinoceros, moose, and snow leopard, but most people were well used to seeing shifted animals in the woods that didn't necessarily belong.

As we rounded the house, we stayed hidden amongst the foliage. I watched in silence as the witches slowly approached. What appeared to be like a heat wave rippled in front of us and suddenly Kade's voice sounded through the connection.

"Now," he spoke.

Shifters, witches, and Onyx Rebels descended on the house. I watched the front doors, while Pax was at the back door. Coltrane was watching one side, while Nova and Scout observed from the sky on the other side.

A scream sounded from inside the house. "Two arrested," Kade said through the connection. "Five children located and safe."

"Shit that was quick," Coltrane chuckled.

It sure was. This had to be one of the easier raids we had done. I watched as two cars rolled up a long dirt road and stop in front of the house. Kade walked outside with one woman cuffed in silver. Her white hair was wild, and her eyes were pure hatred as he placed her in the back of one car. Memphis escorted the other woman out who looked equally livid and placed her in the other car.

"Alright, pack it up, we are bringing the medics to look over the kids before taking them back to the precinct," Kade said through the connection.

I nodded my head and turned to walk out of the forest before shifting back to my human form and getting dressed again. Just as I reached the van, I saw the medic vans arriving. I sent out a small prayer to the universe that the kids would be alright. It was the same prayer I said for every child, that we rescued from one of these hell holes.

Chapter Three

M addox
I was so busy that I had completely forgotten about the school Anghus wanted to build on the Devil's Advocates compound. It had been a hell of a few months. My two jobs turned into four and I had to double my staff. It was great for my bank account but hell for my blood pressure.

"Maddox," Anghus said with a grin. He had a little girl on his shoulders as he ducked through the workshop door.

"Anghus, and the ever-beautiful Miss McKenna. What can I do for the two of you today?" I asked.

Anghus grinned and placed a rolled-up plan on the reception desk. "The architect finalized the plans for the school building."

I nodded and unrolled the plans. It was standard. Basically, it was going to be a building consisting of three rooms, a couple of offices, and a bathroom complex.

"I like it," I said as I looked over the plans. The building would be built not far from where the main house of the community was held. I'd helped to renovate it after it had been sitting abandoned for twenty years. We had to basically gut the entire building and start again. Rats and wildlife had made a bit of a mess in the place. Now though, you'd never know that it had once been left and forgotten. Or that a grisly murder had taken place in that exact building.

"Yeah, this will be the last building to make the compound complete," Anghus said.

I chuckled and looked up at the big gargoyle. "Are you sure?"

Anghus laughed and nodded his head. "Yeah. I'm sure in a few years we will need more housing, with the extra omegas we are always gaining but between the community compound and the other compound we have plenty."

"You are doing great work," I said. I'd always thought the Devil's Advocates were awesome people. But knowing the work they did with omegas really impressed me. They were made of groups of omegas who had been taken from their homes or born into breeding facilities. The lives the omegas had lived were horrific ones. Knowing that there was a group of people out there to help them adjust to a life of freedom was fantastic. To be able to help in part with that, made me feel great.

"Thanks, man. You've done a lot to help us with that," Anghus replied.

I waved my hand and shook my head. It was my honor to help them. I saw it as my way of giving back to the world. Tom and Margaret loved hearing about my jobs with the Devil's Advocates when I rang and chatted to them. I had a lot to be grateful for. I could've ended up being one of those omegas that were taken by breeders.

"Right, so, what is your time frame to get the school up and happening?" I asked.

"Well, that depends on you. I don't want to push you; I know you're a busy man."

I nodded. "One of my crews has just finished a job, so they will be ready to start again next week, they are just doing the finishing touches on the place. So, what if we go out and make a start on the marking and stuff for the foundation, then once the concreters and plumbers have laid what they need to, we will start on the structure?"

"That sounds awesome man," Anghus replied with a wide grin. "I can't wait to see this school up and happening."

"It is such an interesting concept. So, you are only taking supernatural kids?"

Anghus nodded. "Yeah, I guess the opening is there for human kids at some stage, but we want to tailor the education so that the kids learn how to utilize all their powers. We want their powers to be like a second skin."

I hummed. "Who are you going to be having to teach them?"

"At the moment it will be some of the Onyx Rebels. We have tutors for the general stuff, like mathematics and that sort of thing, but for the power work, we will be relying on some of the elder members of Onyx Rebels, Merza from AJE, and Arcadia the dragon shifter. I think even my Mama is keen on teaching as well."

I grinned. "That sounds amazing. I went to a supernatural school, but we weren't taught about our powers. The education-focused more on the history of supernaturals."

"Do you know what the rest of your heritage is? I know that you are a panda shifter, but what else?"

I hummed and scratched at my chin. "I don't really know to be honest. My Papa kicked me out of the house when I was seventeen and I haven't spoken to him or my Mama since then. It wasn't really something that was talked about. My Papa was a panda shifter and Mama was a polar bear shifter."

Anghus nodded his head. "When you come out to the compound, you should talk to Arcadia, she has access to all the records of supernaturals, she will be able to tell you where you descended from, then if you wanted to learn more about your powers, feel free to join in. Us adults are learning as well."

I smiled and nodded emphatically. "I like the sound of that. I will if I get the time. Thanks, man."

Anghus smiled and reached out a hand for me to shake. I placed my hand in his and said our goodbyes before the gargoyle left the workshop and left me with a lot to think about. It would be interesting to know where I came from. I wondered if I had other families out there. Family, I didn't even know. I'd never known Mama's family. Well, from what Papa had told me, I did before it all turned to shit, and I was attacked by one of Mama's brothers. But I wondered if I even wanted to know about the family. Or whether I was just happy to be a panda.

Chapter Four

N^{ash}

I leaned back in my chair and let out a groan. Over the last six months, we had been flat out. It was one after another breeding facility being shut down. Before we ended Morpheus the leaders had their breeding facilities, they were big productions. But now that Morpheus had been officially broken up, those outlier facilities had become smaller operations.

One by one we had been working on shutting them down, but it felt like an endless line of places. Every time we felt like we'd got to the end there would be another setup. So many damned kids. Some taken as early as the 1970s were suddenly being found. It was astonishing. How we hadn't seen it beforehand was beyond me.

But now that the main Morpheus members were either rotting in jail or like Ettore on the run, it brought to light the cases that had long been cold. Our focus was narrowing in. It broke my heart to see the now adults who were taken so many years ago. They were brainwashed, broken, and barely clinging to their sanity. Some of them didn't even remember their real family. They only knew the family that had been created for them through abduction and torture.

The family members of those kids felt the anguish all over again. A time that should have been filled with joy, wasn't. Their child was a shell of the person they had once been. It was devastating to watch. I couldn't even begin to imagine the pain that the families had to be feeling to get the knowledge that their child was now safe, but they were still locked in that world, forever changed.

"What are you getting up to this weekend?" Coltrane asked as he came and flopped down in the seat beside me.

I scrubbed my hands up over my face and ran my fingers through my beard, untangling the knots as I sighed. "I don't know. It feels so weird to have a whole weekend off."

Coltrane chuckled and nodded his head. "Yeah, tell me about it. Monroe said he wasn't sure what he was going to do with me being home all weekend."

I laughed and nodded my head. "Are you and Monroe going to go to KINK?"

Coltrane grinned wickedly at me and nodded emphatically. "Monroe practically demanded it," he said with a laugh. It didn't surprise me, Coltrane's mate, Monroe, was a minx. He loved the kink as much as Coltrane did. There was nothing more exciting for Monroe than being fucked while everyone watched. "What about you? You should come along."

I sighed and shrugged my shoulders. I'd considered going, but the club was holding less appeal to me as time went on. I was a Daddy, there was no denying that. I loved the littles. But lately, I had been craving my own little boy or girl. I knew all the littles at the club, and although they were fun to spend time with, they weren't mine.

"What's up?" Coltrane asked reading the look on my face.

I shrugged my shoulders again. "I don't know. I just have been feeling so discontent lately. I want a little of my own. It's fun to go to the littles room and play. But it's so depressing when I go home, and I don't have a boy or girl to go home with."

Coltrane hummed in his throat and nodded. "I understand. There haven't been any new littles joining lately either."

I nodded. "Yeah. I guess it's just not for me right now."

"When was the last time you played?"

I twisted my lips in thought as I tried to think of the last time I'd played with a little. "God it would be almost a year, I think. It was Ione, at the club."

Coltrane's eyes widened and he shook his head. "Shit, that is so long ago."

I sighed. "Yeah, I know. But I've been so busy, I just haven't really had the time. I just figured if I was supposed to be a Daddy to someone, they would come into my world."

"They will. I'm sure of it."

I smiled over at my friend. I didn't admit it but lately, I'd been feeling so lonely. I'd been craving, not just a little, but just someone. Not for a night or for a quick fuck. I wanted my mate. I wanted someone that I could call mine. Out of the shifter unit, I was the last person that wasn't mated. I was thirty-eight years old, and I didn't want to believe that I wouldn't find my mate, but with every day that passed I started to think that was what was going to happen.

"Hey guys," Bacchus said as he came into the shifter room, holding little McKenna on his hip. Joachim followed in behind him as he chatted to their son Iver. The kids were gorgeous. Iver was wise beyond his years. Like nothing, I'd ever seen before.

"Papa?" Iver said as they came into the room.

Bacchus turned to look at his son. "What's up?"

"We need to invite Nash to the compound on the weekend to help celebrate the opening of the school," Iver said before glancing over at me.

Bacchus frowned at his son and looked up over at me before shrugging his shoulders. "What do you reckon Nash, wanna come?"

I smiled and nodded. "Sure thing. I'll bring some lasagna with me."

"Sounds great," Bacchus said.

"Iver is there something you need to tell Nash?" Joachim asked.

Iver looked at me and grinned. He bit his lips together and shook his head rapidly, causing me to chuckle. Something was going on in that boy's mind, but I didn't know what it was. I just had to trust him. Trust a damned seven-year-old.

"How are those new babies in your family?" Coltrane asked Bacchus.

"They are so gorgeous," Bacchus responded. His brother had just given birth to twins, Thatcher, and Saffron. I hadn't met them yet, but Bacchus had been quick to show us photos. The one thing about the Rigby family, they were so close. It made me think about my own family. My Mama had died when she gave birth to me. Papa had since got mated again, but I and my step mum never saw eye to eye, so I didn't really talk to them often. It was a case of just ringing them once a year at Christmas time.

Chapter Five

Maddox

"Are you going to come out on the weekend to celebrate the finish of the school building with us?" Anghus asked as I watched the painters put on the last coat on the wall of the classroom.

The build had been straightforward and only took us four months from start to finish. I'd been really pleased to see it and the kids who kept a close eye on the build had been exciting to watch. It made me want to sink into my little space so much more.

Something I hadn't done in almost a year because of all the work I'd been doing. It was something I'd held onto since my teen years. I'd admitted it to a few people, one being my therapist and the other my best friend, Carter. My therapist believed it was because of the trauma I had as a child. I'd attended a couple of nights at the kink club, KINK, and seen their little room, with Carter who worked security there. As much as those nights had been fun, they weren't for me. Being a little for me, wasn't about a sexual kink.

For me sinking into my little space was about safety. It was about knowing that no one was going to hurt me, and I guess my therapist was right, it was about taking back some of what I missed out on growing up. My father had been an abusive asshole all my life. I never knew a time when I was allowed to be a kid. So, when I did sink into my little space, I knew it was time for me to just be.

"Yeah, that would be good, what would you like me to bring?" I asked.

Anghus screwed his nose up and shook his head. "Nothing, just yourself."

I barked out a laugh. I had to admit, I wasn't a good cook. In fact, I absolutely sucked at it. The last time I'd attempted to bring cookies for the kids to try out when we were building some of the compounds, I'd mixed the salt up with the sugar. I still hadn't lived that down and no one let me cook after that.

"The guys from the AJE authority will be here with their mates and children, as well as the Rigby Brothers and some of the Onyx Rebels," Anghus informed me.

"Sounds good. How about I bring some soft drink with me?"

Anghus chuckled. "That sounds much safer. Want to bring your crew too? It would be good for everyone to meet them."

I nodded my head and smiled. "Sounds great. I'm sure they will be thrilled to be included. This place has almost become a second home for us."

Anghus grinned. "Good, then we are doing the right thing. That's how I've wanted it to feel. I want people to be comfortable here."

"I'm proud to have been involved. The work you guys do, man, it's amazing."

"Anghus," a little voice called before a little girl with blonde hair and blue eyes ran towards the big gargoyle and leaped into his arms.

Anghus chuckled as he caught the little girl and pressed kisses onto her face. "This is Seven, Larissa and Corson have just adopted her and her sisters and brothers."

"And my Mama," Seven said.

Anghus grinned and nodded his head. "And your Mama."

Seven tucked her head into Anghus's neck and tangled her fingers up into his beard.

"Breeding facility?" I asked nodding my head towards the little girl in his arms.

Anghus sighed and nodded. "Yeah. They've been here just over a month. I wish we had found them a long time ago."

"How many were there?"

"Ten kids all up, but only nine here. One of the kids had been taken and AJE authority hasn't been able to find them. Onyx Rebels are still on the case, but they think she was taken overseas and sold."

I winced, I hated it. The worst atrocities were the breeding facilities.

"There you are, little mermaid," an older girl said with a chuckle.

Seven lifted her head and giggled. "I wanted to cuddle with Anghus."

"I can tell," the older girl laughed before she looked at me warily.

"One, this is Maddox, he is a panda shifter, omega. He is the builder that built the school and basically this whole complex," Anghus introduced.

The girl's frown eased slightly but she didn't smile. I could see that she was wary of me, and I totally understood.

"Hello, One. It's lovely to meet you."

One nodded her head but didn't return the sentiment. She took Seven in her arms, who squealed with giggles and turned back towards the main house where the other children were playing.

"They all have numbers for names?" I asked.

Anghus nodded. "Yeah, the cunts couldn't even give them the dignity to have a normal name. I asked them when they came here if they wanted to change their names, but they didn't. They said that's what they wanted to be called."

"They were all born into the breeding facility?"

Anghus shook his head. "No. One wasn't, she was abducted and brought there, but we still haven't been able to find her parents or where she was taken from. There is a possibility that she was taken from overseas and brought here. But Arcadia and the Onyx Rebels are still researching. Not that I think she would ever want to go back to the family she had before. Seven and Five are her biological children, the others are from another omega, Two."

"Shit," I said with a shake of my head.

"Yeah, it's a fucking disaster. But every day that they spend time here with Larissa and Corson they just seem to come alive."

I nodded and smiled. "This is the best place for them."

Chapter Six

N^{ash}

I bundled the large deep dishes of lasagna that I'd baked that morning into the backseat of my car. The trays took up the whole back seat and onto the floor. There were a lot of Devils to feed. Lasagna was a favorite it seemed, the few times I'd been out there with the guys from work, the kids always asked if I had brought the lasagna. I liked it. I loved it when people ate my food with gusto. It made me feel good about what I'd made. I guess in a way I had a bit of a praise kink maybe.

As I pulled up to the main house of the compound, I was shocked to see just how much work they'd achieved. The place was looking more like a little community rather than a few houses. Kids ran around with huge smiles on their faces. Adults stood around watching them and playing or laughing together. I had often wondered if I would rather live in a community like the Devil's Advocates had.

Sometimes living on my own in my apartment was lonely. I loved being surrounded by people. I loved the idea of helping to keep a community running and having friends that were more like family. Maybe it was some deep-seated trauma thing because I never really grew up with a family that I could rely on.

My driver's door swung open, and I chuckled at the big brown eyes of Iver as he grinned a toothless smile at me.

"Hey, you've lost some more teeth, I see," I said with a grin.

His head bounced up and down. Sometimes it was hard to remember that Iver was a seven-year-old boy. It was easy to get lost in his wisdom. Bacchus said it was because he was cthulu, but I often wondered if it was because he had been on this earth before.

"Did you bring lasagna?" he asked, causing me to laugh.

"I sure did, have a look in the backseat," I said as I climbed out of the driver's side.

Iver pressed his nose against the back window and gasped. "Woah, that must've taken you ages."

"Most of the morning, but remember I love doing it."

Iver grinned up at me and bounced his head up and down. "I'll get Papa and they will be able to help you bring it in."

"Thanks, Iver," I replied as I reached into the back seat for the first tray of lasagna.

"Nash, thank you so much for making this, it smells divine," Joachim said as he stepped in beside me and reached out a tray of lasagna.

Anghus, Bacchus, and a few others came down the stairs and I piled their arms full of trays, once the car was empty, I followed the guys into the main house where most of the inner crew of the Devil's Advocates were seated in the living room with some of the guys from the AJE Authority. Pax and Bacchus both lived on the compound, and I'd heard that Raiden was considering moving out there too.

"Hey Nash," Raiden said with a smile.

I grinned and gave a small wave as I passed through the living room and into the kitchen.

"Want a beer?" Anghus asked as he reached into the fridge and pulled out two cold bottles of beer.

"Yeah, that would be great, thank you," I replied taking the beer out of Anghus's hand once he'd popped the lid off.

"I'm glad you could come out, I feel like we haven't seen you in ages," Joachim said.

"Yeah, it's been a hell of a six months. We've been flat out. I don't think I've had a full night's sleep in forever."

Joachim nodded his head. "Yeah, poor Bacchus has spent more time at the precinct than he has home. I'm just glad you guys have at least the weekend off."

"Me too. How are the kids from the raid settling in?" I asked.

Anghus grinned. "Great. Larissa and Corson have officially adopted them. Michael helped them with the applications and was able to rush it through the courts due to the kid's situation."

"Any luck in finding One's parents?" I asked.

Anghus sighed and shook his head. "No. Scout and Kaki are still trying to find them. Arcadia has done some work with her, with hypnosis. The best we've got is that she came on a plane with a man, she never knew his name."

I winced. "And she doesn't remember where the plane came from?"

Anghus shook his head. "Nope. And Arcadia can't see it, she thinks that the trauma has caused her to block pretty much everything."

"Poor fucking kid. It disgusts me."

"Me too, man. Me too. Anyway, enough shop talk, we are here to celebrate. Wanna come and check out the school?"

I grinned and nodded. "Sure do."

Anghus smiled in return and led me out towards the school building.

Chapter Seven

Maddox

I'd woken up feeling itchy all over. It was like I was due for a heat, but when I looked at my calendar, I realized that I still had another week before I was due. I wondered if perhaps I should cancel going out to the Devil's Advocates compound. Especially if my heat was going to be coming early, I didn't want to be there around alphas. I knew that Anghus would see that I was kept safe, but I wasn't sure.

I was still tossing up whether to go or not when a knock on my door shook me out of my inner thoughts. I swung the door open to the one man that I truly called a friend. He was the only other person that knew about my little side. I kept it well hidden, in closets and in storage boxes.

"Maddox?" Carter said as he looked at me with a frown on his face.

I shook my head. "I don't know what is going on with me."

Carter reached out a big hand and placed it on my forehead. "You're heating up. But you're not due for a heat yet. So, I think you might be getting sick."

I sighed and nodded my head. Carter was used to littles, and people who liked different lifestyles. He, himself was a Dom, who enjoyed some very kinky things.

"I know," I said with a frown.

"Are you sure you should be going out today?"

I sighed and shook my head. "I'm not sure. I don't know that I should be, but I promised I would. I don't want to be a disappointment," I replied with tears welling up in my eyes. That was my biggest fear. Growing up the way I did, I knew that I was a people pleaser. I didn't want anyone to be disappointed in me.

"Oh Maddox, Anghus will understand."

I sighed and the tears that had welled up in my eyes broke down over my cheeks. Carter sighed and pulled me into his arms. He held me tight as I cried. *Why now? Why did I have to get sick now?*

"Would you like me to pop you on the couch with your favorite cartoons? I'll get you your blankie and pacifier," Carter said looking down into my eyes.

I nodded my head and sighed again. This was a disaster. I was going to be letting them down. My crew would go out to the compound, and I was going to be stuck on the couch. I was hopeless. Useless.

"Enough of that," Carter growled, letting out just enough alpha to snap me out of my inner berating.

"How did you know what I was thinking?" I pouted.

Carter chuckled and tapped my nose. "I could see it on your face. Come on little one, let's get you in your jammies, and then I'm going to get you some warm milk and your suppressors just in case you are going into heat early."

"Okay," I mumbled as I let Carter guide me back inside and into my bedroom. He went to my dresser and opened the drawer where I kept my pajamas.

"Diaper, or no?" he asked.

"No, not today," I replied. Sometimes I liked using a diaper, but I wasn't that far into little space that I wanted to be bothered. I just wanted comfort.

"Alright," he said as he pulled out my favorite onesie. It had dinosaurs all over it and made me feel strong and warm whenever I wore it. "Okay little one, arms up."

I stuck my arms up in the air feeling myself drift further into little space the more Carter did for me. He stripped me out of my shirt, before slipping my jeans down off my legs followed by my boxers.

"First leg," Carter instructed as he held my bright red training undies out. I held onto Carter's shoulders as I stepped into the undies, followed by my jammies. Once I was zipped up and dressed, Carter stood and went to my bedside drawer where I kept my bounty of pacifiers. He picked out the green one that matched my jammies and rubbed the nipple against my lips. I opened my mouth and sucked the pacifier in, instantly feeling a calm wash over me.

"Okay little one, let's get you out to the couch and I'll put some cartoons on, then I'm going to make you some warm milk and some sandwiches that you can get when you feel hungry later."

I nodded my head and allowed Carter to lead me over to the couch. I laid down and felt the warmth wrap around me as Carter tucked me under my favorite quilt that Margaret had made me when I first moved out. Carter flicked on the television and found some cartoons and I let my mind drift away as I got lost in watching the action on the screen. Carter brought me a sippy cup with warm milk inside. He handed me a small tablet of a suppressor which I swallowed down with the warm milk. I gave him a smile as he kissed the top of my head with a promise to come back and check me once his shift was over.

I closed my eyes and allowed my body to nap with the cartoons playing in the background, sinking into the safety that my little space held for me.

Chapter Eight

Nash

"Papa," Iver called as he came into the main house. I was just setting out the last tray of lasagna on the bench ready for eating.

"Iver," Joachim answered causing Iver to giggle.

"Maddox isn't here," Iver said with a frown. I knew Maddox by name only, I'd never met the talented carpenter, but had seen his craftmanship. I was always impressed by his work.

"Oh, so he isn't. I'll give him a ring and check that he is alright," Joachim said as he pulled the phone from his pocket. He pressed his phone to his ear as it rang, but the phone rang out. "Hmm. I'll try one more time, maybe he is just running late."

By the second time, the call rang out I could see slight concern marring Joachim's face.

"Something is wrong Papa," Iver said.

Joachim frowned at his son. "Is that you assuming, or is the creator telling you that there is something?"

"The creator," Iver said as he looked over at me. "Nash, will you go to his house and check on him?"

"I can send your dad," Joachim said before I had a chance to answer.

Iver shook his head rapidly. "No. It has to be Nash."

"Oh ok," Joachim responded before looking at me. "Don't feel pressured. You still have a choice, despite what my son thinks."

I nodded my head. "I'm happy to go. I've never met Maddox before, but if the creator is telling Iver something is wrong, then I want to help."

I glanced down at Iver who was watching me with a small frown pulling at his brow. The way his eyes roved side to side I could see that he wasn't focusing on me. He was communicating with someone. Suddenly he blinked and looked at me clearly.

"Nash," he said before crooking his finger beckoning me to go closer to him. I crouched and leaned in. "Maddox isn't like other men, he has a secret that not many people know, but the creator says you'll understand, but Maddox will be embarrassed."

I frowned, not completely understanding what he meant. "Do you know what the secret is?"

Iver shook his head. "No, the creator said that it wasn't for me to know."

I nodded. "Alright, is there anything I should take with me?"

Iver nodded and smiled. "Some lasagna."

I chuckled and ruffled the boy's hair. "Alright, then I'll do that."

"Thank you, Nash," Joachim said. "I'll let Anghus know that you've gone to check on Maddox, he will understand. I just hope it's nothing too major going on."

"I'll let you know when I know," I replied.

Joachim smiled and handed me a plate with some lasagna on it. He quickly jotted down Maddox's home address for me. I knew that Maddox was an omega. I went over and over what it could be that was wrong.

"Nash," Iver called as I reached my car. I turned to look at the little boy. "His spare key is taped to the bottom of his letterbox."

I smiled and nodded. "Thank you, Iver."

Iver grinned and waved at me. During the drive over to Maddox's house, I continued to wrack my mind as to what could be wrong. I was also very curious about what his secret could be and whether that would have something to do with what was wrong with him. Iver was certainly a talented boy.

As I pulled up in front of Maddox's house, I noticed that there was a car still in the driveway, which I assumed belonged to the panda shifter. I hummed in my throat in thought, there didn't appear to be any other sign of life in the house. The blinds were pulled low. I grabbed the plate of food and walked up the driveway to the front door.

I pressed on the doorbell and listened. I thought I could hear voices from the inside, but I couldn't hear what was being said. I pressed my ear to the door and brought my moose closer to the front so that I could enhance my hearing. The voices continued and I quickly worked out that it was a television that I could hear.

I rang the doorbell again and listened, but there was still no movement from inside. I turned and looked for the letterbox that sat next to the door. Reaching beneath it, I felt for the key that Iver said would be taped there. Sure enough, my fingers felt over the metal of the key. Untapping it, I pushed the key into the lock and felt the door unlock. Twisting the knob, I pushed the door open.

"Maddox?" I called before walking into the front foyer. "It's Nash, from the AJE Authority. Iver sent me, he was worried about you."

The television played on but there was no other sound. I stepped in through the front door and gasped. My eyes widened. Mate. Oh my god. I found my mate. I followed the sound of the television into the living room and stopped dead in the doorway.

There tucked up in a dinosaur onesie with a pacifier in his mouth was my little boy. My mate. Maddox. I chuckled. The universe sure had a sense of humor. Quietly I walked through the room until I reached the kitchen and placed the lasagna on the bench. Walking back into the living room I glanced down at my boy. His face was red, and his hair was stuck to his forehead with sweat. I reached out a hand and stroked it over his cheek. Maddox moaned. He was burning up.

"It's alright little one, you're sick," I said quietly.

Maddox's eyes flicked open; they were glazed. "I hurt."

"I know baby. Let's get you into a cool bath to get the temperature down," I said quietly.

"Who are you?" Maddox said seeming to realize for the first time that a stranger was standing in his house.

"My name is Nash. I'm a detective with the AJE Authority. I was at the Devil's Advocate compound, Iver sent me, he said that there was something wrong," I explained.

Maddox nodded his head. "I feel," he said before he quickly rolled to the side of the couch and promptly barfed all down the front of me. He wiped his hand over his mouth and looked up at me with horror. "I'm so sorry."

I chuckled. "It's alright little one. Come on let's get you cleaned up and then Daddy, I mean, I will need to shower."

Maddox giggled. "Daddy. You *are* my Daddy."

I chuckled. "We will talk about that when you are feeling better."

Maddox bounced his head up and down. I could tell that he was still floating in between adult space and little space. It wasn't time to discuss our mating. Not while he wasn't feeling well. I helped Maddox to stand and lead me into the bathroom where I got a cool bath ready for him.

"Do you want me to step out while you bathe?" I asked.

Maddox shook his head. "No."

I nodded and helped the boy out of his jammies. Testing the water, I made sure it wasn't too cold, I held his hand as he climbed into the bath. Taking the wash cloth, I washed him over. Maddox shivered as the cool water hit his back. Once he'd been in the water long enough to start pruning, I helped him to climb out and dried him before directing him to take me to his bedroom.

"Which drawer do you keep your jammies in?" I asked.

Maddox pointed to the right drawer in his dresser, and I pulled it open. Next to the jammies were neatly stacked diapers. I tossed up whether to just put one on him or not. Deciding that it would be better for him to have one if he wasn't feeling good, I pulled out the diaper and powder, along with a pair of jammies.

"Alright little man, lay up on the bed and let me get you ready for bed," I directed.

Maddox nodded his head and sleepily laid on the bed. I slipped the diaper under his hips and smothered him in powder before wrapping the diaper across his waist. I could see Maddox slipping deeper into little space by the time he had his jammies on and was ready for bed.

"I'm going to get you some pain relief, that will help with the fever too," I said as I tucked him into bed and tucked the stuffy that he had sitting on his bed, under his chin.

"Thank you," Maddox murmured. "Nash?"

I turned at the doorway and looked at my boy. "Yeah?"

"You're my mate."

I grinned and nodded my head. "Yeah, I am baby. No rush yet. Let's get you better first."

Maddox smiled and nodded his head before he stuck his thumb in his mouth and closed his eyes. I went into the living room to clean up the vomit and find him some pain relief. My mate. Iver the cheeky monkey knew all along. I chuckled and shook my head. That kid.

Chapter Nine

M addox
I didn't remember how I made it to my bed when I opened my eyes what felt like hours later. The bedroom was dark and when I looked down at my body, I realized I was in different jammies. And I had a diaper on. Carter hadn't put a diaper on me when he laid me on the couch. *Did I do that myself?*

I tried to think back, I felt hot and itchy when Carter came, he gave me a heat suppressor and laid me on the couch. *Then what?* I gasped as I remembered Daddy. *Was it real? Did I really have a mate here? A Daddy?* A vision of him bathing me in cool water and telling me it would reduce my fever. I had brief glimpses of him coming into the room and giving me sips of water, checking my temperature, and changing my diaper when I soiled myself.

With a trembling hand, I flipped the blanket off my body. Only Carter had ever seen me in little space. I would be mortified if someone else saw me. I was fully in adult space now and slowly crept out of the bedroom into the living room where I could hear the television playing lightly. The light from the television cast shadows against the wall. The room was dark as I crept in. I gasped, quickly placing my hands over my mouth as I looked down on the couch at the man who I'd called Daddy. He was asleep on the couch with the remote in his hand.

"Shit," I said quietly as I breathed in. He was my mate. Holy shit. What the fuck was I going to do with that.

The man on the couch groaned and his eyes blinked open before I had a chance to duck out of the room to the safety of my room.

"Little one, you're awake," the man said, his voice was deep and husky from being woken. "How are you feeling?"

"Um, much better. I'm not in little space now," I said.

The man nodded and sat up. "Do you remember much?" I shook my head and bit into my bottom lip. "That's alright. My name is Nash

Andrews. I'm a detective with the AJE authority. I was at the Devil's Advocates compound, well two days ago. Anyway, Iver said that he felt something was wrong with you and insisted that I come and check on you. So, I came."

"How did you get in?" I asked wondering if I'd forgotten to lock the door.

"Iver told me where you kept the spare key."

I shook my head. I didn't even know how to comprehend how Iver knew where I kept my spare key.

"You looked after me," I said as I sat down on the couch beside Nash.

Nash nodded his head. "I did. You were very sick. Between vomiting a few times and a fever, you slept most of the two days."

"I thought I was going into heat early," I muttered.

"Yeah, Carter called in and said that he had thought that too and had given you a heat suppressor, but I think it was a tummy bug."

"Carter saw you here?"

Nash chuckled and nodded. "Yeah. He wasn't very happy. I know him from the club. But once I explained to him everything, I just told you, he was alright."

"Oh, you go to the club. That's why you weren't worried about my little space."

Nash nodded. "That's right. I'm a Daddy. I have been for many years. I went to the club, but I haven't been in a long time."

"Being little isn't a sexual kink for me, that's why I'm not a member there."

Nash smiled and nodded. "That's alright. For a lot of littles, it's not about sex. It's about protection and safety."

I nodded my head. "You are really my mate?"

"Yeah baby, but only if you want me to be."

I barked out a laugh. "Are you crazy? Of course, I want to be your mate. I would never turn my back on Mother fate."

Nash grinned and reached out a hand to take mine. We linked our fingers and just looked at each other. The heat suppressor meant I could sit with Nash without going into heat. It would keep working for at least a week before it wore off.

"How about we give it a bit longer first, just to make sure you are well. You already vomited on me twice," Nash chuckled.

My face blushed with embarrassment. "Oh my god. I'm so sorry."

Nash laughed again and shook his head. "No need to be sorry, you couldn't help it."

I gasped and my eyes widened. "You changed my diaper."

Nash nodded. "I did. You were in a bit of a mess and didn't have the energy to change it yourself."

"You weren't grossed out?"

Nash frowned but shook his head. "Of course not. That is part of having a little. Some don't use diapers, but the ones that do, it is part of being a Daddy."

I relaxed back on the couch and chuckled to myself. I couldn't believe it. Of all the men in the world to be mated to. Mother fate had outdone herself.

Chapter Ten

N ash

By the time that Sunday night had rolled around, and Maddox was still asleep, I'd texted Kade to let him know that I wasn't going to be at work the following day. I explained that I met my mate and left it at that. Of course, I received a text from Coltrane immediately asking if what he'd heard was true.

I'd simply texted him back a confirmation. Carter had come on Saturday night to check on Maddox, and when he found me in the house, I swore the big bear was going to become full grizzly and kill me. I'd managed to calm him down with my explanation of how I found myself at Maddox's home. Once Carter checked on Maddox and saw that he was indeed untouched and asleep, he relaxed, and we had a good chat.

Carter had told me that Maddox didn't show his little side to anyone. I was alright with that. Everyone knew I was a Daddy, but it was only Coltrane and those at the club that knew I preferred littles. Everyone else didn't put too much weight into it.

I'd been somewhat startled when I saw Maddox standing in the living room, early Tuesday morning. It took me a few moments to catch up where I was. His face wasn't sweating, and his fever looked like it had finally broken. I'd had to change a few soiled diapers as the poor boy wasn't even awake enough to comprehend what was going on. It never bothered me; this was just some of the less glamourous parts of being a Daddy.

Now he was snuggled up against me on the couch as I stroked my fingers through his hair. I'd turned the early morning cartoons on for him and watched as he instantly sunk back into little space. It made me wonder how often he got a chance to be little with living on his own. I wondered if Carter had been safety for him previously.

Maddox had been quick to explain that being little for him wasn't a sexual kink, which Carter had already told me. I didn't know all of Maddox's story as Carter wasn't willing to divulge, but from what I could tell he came from a horrible home and didn't have much of a childhood. For Maddox being little was about healing from those past hurts and having the chance to be a child, safely. I wanted to honor that.

"You ready to try and eat something, little one?" I asked.

Maddox looked up at me with bleary eyes from watching the television in the low morning light and popped his thumb from his mouth. He bounced his head up and down on his shoulders.

"I don't want to be a grown-up yet," he said in a small voice.

I smiled and kissed the top of his head. "There is no hurry. We don't have to go anywhere today, so it can be a little day."

Maddox smiled and nodded rapidly again. "I like that."

"Okay, good. I'll go and make you something light to eat, I don't want you feeling sick. I think Carter will probably come in later in the morning to see if you are still okay."

Maddox giggled and sighed. "Carter is my best friend."

I chuckled. "He sure is. He looks after you very well."

"Will you look after me too?"

"If that is what you want, then absolutely."

Maddox bounced his head up and down again. "Yep, that's what I want. I want a Daddy who is going to be always with me and look after me so I can go into little space whenever I want."

"I would be honored to be your Daddy. That is something we are going to have to talk about when you are feeling like you want to be in an adult space though. Now isn't the time. Now is the time to put some food in your grumbly belly."

Maddox giggled and pulled his legs up on the couch, wrapping his arms around his knees and rocking to the side. I chuckled as I stood and watched him stretch out on the couch, wriggling his toes and raising his hands above his head in a big yawn. The poor boy was still weary from his sickness.

I went into the kitchen; I'd dashed out yesterday to grab some food that would sit easily in Maddox's belly as well as popping home so I could grab some spare clothes. As it turned out Maddox vomited on two outfits, that I had to wash and wait for to dry. I'd done a load of Maddox's laundry too. It seemed my boy was a projectile vomiter when sick.

Pulling out the fresh bread I'd bought from the bakery and some avocado, I set about making avocado toast with honey. I knew it would be something that would fill his tummy but wouldn't make him feel too sick.

By the time I'd smashed the avocados onto the toast with honey and walked back into the living room, my boy was curled up and asleep. His thumb sucked in between his lips, as his dark lashes caressed his cheeks.

"Maddox, sit up for me baby, try and have something to eat, then I'll change you and pop you back to bed."

Maddox groaned but sat up and opened his eyes with a slow blink. "I need to wee."

I chuckled. "Want to go do that and then come back and eat some toast?"

"Yep," Maddox replied with a pop of p. He dashed off the couch and beelined for the bathroom. I could hear him muttering as he obviously fumbled with the diaper before I heard the trickle of his urine hitting the toilet. As soon as I heard the toilet flush and the water in the basin run, I watched the hallway, to see my boy running down with no pants on.

"Maddox? Did you forget something?" I asked.

Maddox frowned and looked down at himself before he started to laugh. "Yep," he replied as he quickly dashed and ran for the bathroom.

No sooner had it felt like he left, and he was back again, this time with his pajama pants back on.

"Alright baby, come sit down and have some toast," I directed.

Maddox sat on the couch beside me and took the plate of Avocado toast that I'd cut into small squares from my hands. He picked up the first piece and bit into it before humming. "This is so good. I've never had this before."

I smiled. "I'm glad you like it."

"You're the best cook ever."

I think I could get used to that.

Chapter Eleven

M addox
After breakfast, Nash sorted me out another bath. I was a bit embarrassed this time, especially since I was still floating between little and adult space, but I also wasn't quite with it the last time he bathed me. As it turned out he was good. My bath was done run of the mill. He washed me, methodically and was careful to not make anything sexual. When my cock did stir, he ignored it and just washed down another area of my body. I really appreciated it. I knew that if he belonged to KINK then he knew a lot about rules and the difference between a little kink and a little lifestyle.

Once I was in fresh pajamas and Nash put my bedding in the washing machine, we were sitting watching more cartoons. I was sitting on the floor cross-legged, coloring in one of my favorite books, while Nash watched me. The front door swung open, and I looked up to see Carter coming in through the front door.

"Carter," I said with a smile.

"Hey little man," Carter replied. "You look like you are feeling a lot better."

"Yep. But I'm not ready to be grown up yet."

Carter flicked a quick glance up at Nash who smiled and nodded his head. "That's okay. But I'm sure that Nash and you are going to have to have an adult talk soon, Nash is going to have to go back to work."

I sighed and sat back against the couch. "When?" I asked.

Carter looked over at Nash. "Tomorrow," Nash answered sadly.

"So, I need to be a grown-up, huh?" I said feeling myself being pulled out of little space quickly. There were conversations to be had. Important conversations. If Nash was to be my mate, he needed to understand everything about my little side, and I needed to understand who Nash was as a Daddy.

"Yeah, sorry little man," Carter replied.

I nodded my head and sighed. "Alright. I'll be back in a minute; I can't do adult conversations in pajamas." I stood on the floor and went into the bedroom to put on a fresh pair of sweats and a t-shirt.

Once I'd changed and came back into the living room, I saw that Nash and Carter had cleaned away my little stuff and the living room was back to looking like an adult space again. I sat down on the couch and smiled over at Nash. Now that I was looking at him with adult eyes, I saw what a handsome man he was. His skin was tanned like he spent a lot of time in the outdoors, his dark hair curled around his ears and his chin was covered in a thick dark beard. He looked at me with brown eyes that seemed to bore into my soul.

"What are you thinking Maddox?" Nash asked.

"That you're hot," I said feeling my cheeks blush with my admission.

Nash's eyes flared with heat as a small smile crept across his lips. "I think you're hot too."

I waved my hand and shook my head. "Na, I'm pudgy in the middle."

"I happen to be very fond of pudgy in the middle," Nash rebutted causing me to laugh.

"Alright, you two. Now that I've seen that you're better and in the right mind, I'll head out so the two of you can talk," Carter said breaking into our conversation.

I looked over at my friend with a smile. He stood from the seat he'd been sitting in and stepped forward pressing a quick kiss to the top of my head.

"Thank you for looking out for me," I said looking up at the big bear shifter.

"Always. Don't leave anything unsaid."

I nodded my head as I understood the meaning. I needed to explain to Nash exactly why I needed my little space. I needed to let him into all my dark spots. The only other person I'd ever let in before was Carter. I'd thought for a while that maybe Carter could be my Daddy, but Carter had sat me down and explained that while he was dominant, he wasn't the right Dom for me. He wasn't a Daddy.

I'm glad he did that. If I had mated with Carter, I would never have met Nash. I glanced over at my mate who was watching me with a small smile on his face. Carter gave me a wave as he stepped out of my front door and shut it behind him with a click.

"So, who wants to start?" I asked.

"Why don't you first tell me what you need from a Daddy?" Nash replied.

I sucked in a deep breath and nodded my head. "I can do that."

Nash smiled and shuffled on the couch to make himself more comfortable.

Chapter Twelve

N ash
  I knew that whatever Maddox was planning to tell me was going to be bad. Carter hadn't told me much but had warned that Maddox hadn't had a good life. Maddox fidgeted with his fingers as he sat beside me, not making eye contact.

"Whatever you need to tell me, baby, I promise you that I will never judge you, never," I said quietly.

Maddox took a shaky breath and bounced his head up and down. When he did glance up, I saw the tears that had gathered on his lower lashes. It tore at my heart, knowing that someone had caused those tears. Someone had taken Maddox's heart and ripped it apart.

"I was born as the only child to my parents. My father, Joseph Chan, and my mother Erica. My father was a Chinese immigrant. He came to Australia as a child with his parents. His parents had escaped China, they were poor and had come many years ago. My mother came from a wealthy family, her family was the Tesslar's."

"Oh," I said as I nodded my head. I knew of the Tesslar's. Everyone in Australia did. They were a very well-known family involved in politics and mining.

"Anyway, I don't know how it came to be, but my grandfather met my mother's father, and they became friends. Papa never spoke much about what happened, but all I know is that some deal was brokered, and Papa was betrothed to Mama."

I nodded as I listened to Maddox tell his story. "I was born not long after their mating. They were never fated to be mates apparently. It was something that Mama always resented. Papa was happy because it gave him access to Mama's wealth. Anyway, when I was three, one of Mama's brothers came to stay with us. I don't remember him very well. But from the stories I've heard and read online, he was not a nice man. As it turned out the stories were true. Larry raped me at three years old.

At first, he wasn't caught, it wasn't until one day Papa came home early and discovered his brother-in-law in my bedroom raping me and Mama sitting in the living room ignoring everything."

"Papa was furious. He beat Larry badly. Larry had to have some major surgery to survive. Mama's family didn't believe Papa because I had no damage to me. But what they didn't know is that while Papa was beating Larry, Mama had told me to shift so that all my wounds were healed. I don't really remember any of it. Therapists told me that I blocked it all out. But Mama's family was so angry that Papa would tell such a story about their son and then beat him so badly that they cut Papa out. Mama was given the choice to leave the mateship and go back home or to stay with Papa, but she wouldn't have her family anymore. Mama always said that she wanted to go home, but Papa demanded that she stay as punishment for letting her brother hurt me. Papa was furious that he no longer had access to the money. Mama's family told everyone to never trust the Chan family. Mama and Papa's parents fell out over it. Papa in turn blamed me for what Larry did to me. As a result, he beat me repeatedly. Told me I was a disappointment, and I was unclean and disgusting."

I shook my head as I listened to the story that Maddox told me. It was ripping me apart. I wanted to hunt down Larry and tear him to shreds, I wanted to do the same to Maddox's family.

"When I was seventeen, I was accepted into trade school to become a carpenter. Papa was so angry. He didn't want me to become a tradesman. He wanted me to go on to something better in his eyes, a doctor or a lawyer, something that would boost the Chan name, once more. I refused him and he beat me, kicking me out of the house."

"Shit, baby, I'm so fucking sorry that you went through all of that," I said as I gently reached out a hand to take Maddox's in mine.

Maddox looked up at me and gave me a weak smile. "I was lucky. The night Papa kicked me out I'd just taken off, running like lightning. Somehow when I finally stopped, I had stopped in front of my woodwork teacher's home. Tom Beard. He and his wife took me in. They treated me like family, they got me in to see a therapist and became more like a mum and dad than what my Mama and Papa ever were."

I smiled and stroked my thumb over Maddox's hand. I was so glad that he had found someone to rely on. And when I got to finally meet Tom and his wife, I would be thanking them for what they did.

"My therapist believes that the reason I like being in little space is that my childhood was robbed for me. This is my way of controlling my childhood in a sense. Even though I don't remember what Larry did to me, somewhere in my psyche it is still there and the fact that Papa brought it up as often as he could to blame me, affected me."

I nodded. "I can imagine it did. But it also explains why being little for you isn't a kink. You were hurt as a child sexually. Anything sexual, while you are in little space, would trigger you."

Maddox looked up at me and smiled again. "You *do* understand."

I grinned. "I do. As soon as I realized that I liked littles and that I was a Daddy, I did a lot of research into everything."

Maddox chuckled. "Mother fate."

I smiled again and leaned over to press a small kiss on Maddox's cheek. "She knew what she was doing."

$$\mathbf{M}^{\text{addox}}$$

I felt a sense of relief when I finished telling Nash about my life. The look on his face told me that he didn't judge me or even pity me. He understood. He realized why I was a little, but not in the kink sense. It made me feel good that Mother fate had picked him for me. I couldn't have asked for a better mate to have.

"Tell me about you?" I asked.

Nash smiled and nodded. "My story isn't as impactful as yours. My Mama died when she was giving birth to me. I lived with just my Papa until I was thirteen and then he remated. His mate though didn't like me. She felt resentful that Papa had a mate before her and a child that belonged to another woman. They had four more children, but I left home when I was seventeen. I went to university and my Papa sort of just stopped communicating with me. I tried to ring him a few times while I was at university, but he never bothered to reach out. When no one attended my graduation, I got the message. Now and then I get the odd Christmas card from them, but it's only to tell me of something great that one of my siblings have done. I try to call Papa every year at Christmas but our conversations only last about thirty seconds. Long enough to say Merry Christmas to one another and that's it."

I winced and screwed up my nose. "That's shitty. I hate that for you."

Nash shrugged his shoulders. "It is what it is. I was hurt for a long time when I was a kid, but I've come to accept it as it is and moved on."

"Do you not have anything to do with your siblings?" I asked.

Nash shook his head. "No, my step mum poisoned them against me. They were told I was this big bad man who had turned his back on his Papa and destroyed his heart. It wasn't true, but they had no reason not to believe their mother."

"She's a bitch. How old are your siblings now?"

"Thalia would be twenty-six, she was born when I was fourteen and then there is Russell who is twenty-two, Lacey is eighteen, and Lily who've I've never met is twelve."

"I wish I could change it for you. I hate that you don't have family in your life."

Nash shrugged his shoulders. "I built my own family. Like you had with Tom and his wife, I gathered a family with the other shifter unit members and the guys at the club."

I shrugged and nodded. "I guess that's true. Sometimes our adopted families are better to us and for us than our blood relations."

Nash smiled and nodded in response. "That's true. Did Tom and his wife, you didn't tell me her name, have children?"

"Oh yeah, her name is Margaret. They have two children, Allison, and Alexander. They are both older than me. They're humans. Allison is married to a man named Jake and they have one daughter named Isabelle. Alexander is married to a lady named Shania. They don't have any children."

"Do you see them regularly?"

I nodded and smiled. "Yep. I try to go and have a meal with the whole family once a month. Allison and Alexander come to dinner with their family too and we all catch up. Even though I was never biologically related or even human, they always just welcomed me. I can't wait for them to be able to meet you."

"Will they think it's weird that we are mated rather than married?"

I shook my head. "Not at all. At first, it took Tom and Margaret a little bit to get used to the fact that I was supernatural and that we did things a little differently. But Tom had been working in a supernatural predominant school for years. They caught on fast and were very open and understanding."

"That's awesome. I'm glad you had them in your life."

"They'll be in your life too. Margaret doesn't let anyone she meets be a stranger," I chuckled.

Nash grinned. "That sounds fun."

"So, what happens now?" I asked as I bit into my bottom lip.

Nash looked at me and I was positive that I saw his eyes heat as he took me in. "I guess that depends on what you want."

"What do you mean?"

"Well, I mean, we can mate and connect. Or we can take a few days for you to decide if you want me. I want you to be sure because I'm not willing to go through breaking the mateship if you change your mind."

I frowned and shook my head. "No. I don't want to back out. Mother fate brought you to me for a reason. You're mine. I want to mate with you."

Nash's smile was golden as he clasped my hand tighter in his and stood, pulling me up from the couch and leading me into the bedroom that he'd redressed with fresh linen. If I had my way, we were going to be making them very dirty again. But this time in a much more fun way.

Chapter Fourteen

Nash

I kept hold of Maddox's hand as I led him into his bedroom. Before I did anything I needed to know where his mind was. We were going to need more in-depth conversations about when he wants to be little and when not. I will need to know his boundaries. I never want to overstep things and add to any trauma.

"Where is your mind right now?" I asked as I took hold of his other hand as well.

"I'm completely adult right now. I am horny and want to become your mate."

I chuckled at his answer. "That's enough for me. Just know that we stop on your word."

"Do I need a safe word?"

I shook my head. "Unless you really want one, but if you say no or stop then I will honor that immediately, no matter how deep into things we are."

Maddox smiled up at me and bounced his head up and down. "Will you kiss me now?"

Chuckling I closed the space between us and pressed my lips against his. I swept my tongue between his teeth and tangled mine with his. Maddox moaned and he dropped his hold on my hands as he wrapped his arms around my back, clawing at my shirt. I felt his claws lengthen as he shredded the back of my shirt. My eyes flung open, and he looked up at me with a tinge of pink touching his cheeks.

"Sorry, I got excited," he said.

I laughed and pressed a quick kiss against his lips. "Perfectly fine."

I reached for the hem of Maddox's shirt and lifted it up over his head. Although I'd seen him naked already, I wasn't looking at him as a sexual being, but as a little who needed help. He'd gotten half hard in the bath when I washed him, but I'd purposely ignored it. He was in little space at the time and there was no way I was going to take him out of that space.

Now, however, was a different story. Now I took my time in perusing every part of Maddox. He was sexy. He wasn't hard muscles but had a soft layer of flesh that covered the muscles that came from hard work. Maddox ran his hands up over my chest and tangled his fingers in the hair that coated my chest.

"You are so fucking beautiful," he groaned.

"As are you," I replied.

Maddox smiled and blushed. I reached for the waist of his sweatpants and slipped them down over his hips. His cock bounced against his stomach before sticking straight out. Maddox stepped out of the pants that sat around his ankles and pulled at the button on my jeans. Once they were unzipped, I wriggled my legs, as they fell to my feet. Maddox hooked his fingers into the waist of my boxers and slipped them down.

He licked his lips as he looked down at my cock which was hard and throbbing. "Oh my god, you're huge," he whispered.

I didn't think I was anything more than average. I admitted that I was thicker than Maddox, but we were about the same length. He tentatively reached out a hand and stroked it over the hardened shaft. I hissed over my teeth at the feel of his warm hand on my dick. It had been so long since I'd felt anything other than my own hand that the feeling of Maddox was exhilarating.

The scent of Maddox's slick filled the air as he lowered to his knees. He ran his nose up my thighs, to the crease of my hips. He flicked his tongue over my balls. My head rolled back on my shoulders, and I groaned as I thrust my fingers through Maddox's hair. He opened his lips wide and sucked me down over his tongue.

"Fuck, yes, baby," I groaned as he swirled his tongue over the head, lapping at me like it was the most delicious meal he'd ever had. The sounds he made as he bobbed up and down on my shaft made my balls tighten. "Baby you need to stop, it's been a long time and I'm as horny as all hell. If you don't stop, I'm going to cum and I don't want to do that in your mouth. Yet."

Maddox chuckled and placed his hands on my thighs, with another quick flick of his tongue along the underside of my shaft he stood and walked over to the bed. He climbed to the center and kneeled. Widening his thighs, he opened himself completely to me. Maddox leaned forward and pressed his face into the mattress before reaching behind him to grab hold of his ass cheeks and spreading them wide. His hole was coated with slick and was open, ready to be filled.

I groaned before I leaned forward, swiping my tongue through his crease up to his hole. I pushed my tongue inside him, lapping at all the honey that he gave me. Maddox let out a long moan and thrust his hips back against my face. I continued to lick at him, it was something that I couldn't get enough of.

"Nash, please, I need more," Maddox moaned.

I leaned up and grabbed hold of his hips, I twisted him on the bed so that he was on his back. Maddox gasped and looked up at me with wide eyes. I leaned forward and pressed my lips onto his. Maddox groaned and tangled his tongue with mine as I gently thrust forward running my cock along his crease. Maddox lifted his legs and curled them around my waist.

Each time the head of my cock slid over his hole; Maddox moaned. Every sound he made was the sexiest thing I'd ever heard. I guided my cock to his entrance and slowly started to push forward. Maddox gasped, but his eyes rolled in his head as I bottomed out inside him.

Slowly I rolled my hips, making sure the head of my cock ran over his prostate with every thrust. My knot started to form, and my incisors lengthened.

"Do you want me, baby?" I asked.

"Fuck yes," Maddox cried just as he opened his mouth wide and leaned forward. I roared as his teeth penetrated the skin on my chest. My knot locked in place, and I filled my mate full of my seed.

Bending forward I returned the mating bite, sealing us forever. My mate. My man. In human terms, my husband.

Chapter Fifteen

Maddox

"Well hello boss," Carl said as I came into the workshop the following morning.

"Carl," I said with a wide grin.

Carl chuckled. "Alright spill. Who are they?"

I threw my head back and laughed. "His name is Nash. He works for the AJE authority."

"I know Nash, he is a good guy," Carl said before a frown pulled at his brow. "Um, Maddox, look, has Nash told you about his, um, likes?"

My cheeks tinted pink, and I nodded my head before I cleared my throat. "If you are talking about the fact that he is a member of KINK, then yes, I know."

Carl breathed out. "Alright, that's cool. I just wanted to make sure you knew. I thought he'd tell you."

I didn't know a whole lot about Carl. I didn't really socialize with the guys on my crew outside of work.

"Thank you. I appreciate the heads up anyway," I replied.

Carl smiled and nodded his head. "All good. So, what's on the agenda for today?" he asked changing the subject. I was grateful that Carl was prepared to drop the subject. I didn't want my crew knowing that I was a little.

"I've got a meeting with a client for a renovation. Crew A is still working on the Lance house, and Crew B should have made a start on the new build-out on Knox Road. I've got another new job out on Tomlinson Road, so I'll get you and Brandt to come with me for that so we can see the plot."

Carl nodded his head. "Sounds good. How hard is it going to be to get trucks into Tomlinson Road, I know that it is just a gravel road in the middle of the woods isn't it?"

I hummed as I pulled up the maps on my phone. "Shit, yeah, it is."

Carl and I got lost in planning a route that would suit trucks bringing in equipment that all thoughts of my mating were lost. Nash and I hadn't really discussed much beyond our mating. There was a short conversation about whether Nash would move into my home, or I would move in with him, but nothing was set in concrete yet.

By the time Brandt arrived at work, Carl and I were ready to head out to the new plot. This was a new client, one that none of us had heard of before. Not that, that was unusual. We often got new people buying into Lalbert because of the low land prices.

"Who are the owners?" Brandt asked as we drove out in the work van towards Tomlinson Road.

"Archie and Elizabeth Rose," I replied. "They aren't someone that I know."

Carl shook his head. "Yeah, I've never heard of them. They must be new in town."

"We've had a few new faces coming into Lalbert," Brandt said.

I nodded my head and looked out over the scenery. It didn't surprise me that new people came to Lalbert. The place was beautiful. Surrounded by a forest that was filled with thick redgums. Ferns and bracken interspersed the trees. We weren't that far from the ocean; a river ran through one edge of Lalbert. We had everything that was needed to make living here convenient. It was the perfect place for both humans and the supernatural.

"It will be interesting to see whether they are human or supernatural," Brandt said, breaking into my thoughts. "I've heard that we've had heaps of new supernatural's moving here."

"Yeah?" I said with a shake of my head. "I hadn't noticed."

"Well, you wouldn't have over the last few days," Brandt snorted, making me chuckle.

"In my defense, I was sick for the first few days."

"Oh, that sucks. So, the mating mark on your chest didn't happen until recently?"

I laughed. "Yesterday."

Brandt wolf-whistled. "Alright, tell me all about them."

I cast a quick glance over at Carl, who had his eyes focused on the road in front of him as he drove. "His name is Nash. He is a moose shifter."

"A moose and a panda. I wonder what your children will be," Brandt mused.

I didn't even think about children. I stroked my hand down over my belly. There was a high likelihood that I was going to be pregnant. A smile formed on my lips. I didn't care what kind of supernatural I had. If they were born healthy, that's all I hoped for. I would love them regardless. They would have a much better childhood than my own.

Chapter Sixteen

N^{ash}

"Hey," Coltrane said with a wide grin.

"Hello," I greeted as I bit at my cheeks to hide the grin that wanted to spread across my lips.

Coltrane rolled his eyes. "Don't play coy, it's written all over your face. So, Maddox huh?"

I chuckled and nodded my head. "Yep. I'm a mated man."

"Congratulations man. Is he everything you want?" Coltrane asked.

I didn't want to betray Maddox's trust, so I just nodded my head. Coltrane seemed to be able to see the look on my face. He lived by the same rules that I did. It wasn't our place to out anyone. We both knew that Maddox didn't belong to the club which meant the likelihood he wasn't out. I knew he wasn't, but Coltrane didn't.

"That's great, man. We will have to have you and Maddox over. Monroe would love to meet him."

I smiled. "That sounds great."

"Here he is," Pax said as he came into the room and wrapped an arm around my shoulder. "Looking good man."

"Thank you. Let's hope we don't have a litter as you did," I said with a laugh.

Pax threw his head back and laughed. "I keep trying to talk Holland into having more, he thinks I'm crazy. What can I say, I love my kids."

"Aurora and Harper are going to be popping out kids soon enough, then you can focus on being grandpa," I replied.

Pax grinned. "Aurora met her mate at university. Thankfully it happened in her last year. But she is very happy."

"That's awesome man. I'm happy for her. Is her mate a good person?"

Pax nodded. "From what I've seen he is nice. A penguin shifter. Real meek like her. He changed uni's can you believe it. He is studying the same as Aurora, but he decided that he needed to change uni's. The first day there, he meets Aurora."

"Mother fate," I said with a laugh and a shake of my head.

"Yep, that's what we told Aurora. At first, she wasn't totally sure that she should go through with her mating. As you can imagine, Harper had a lot to say on the matter."

I chuckled. Harper was a force to be reckoned with. That girl was a firecracker. She had strong opinions and had no fear. She would do well with Freya as a Domme, I always thought. My phone buzzed in my pocket, and I slipped it out looking at the screen with a frown when I saw that it was my Papa's number ringing.

"Papa?" I answered.

"Nash, thank god you still have this number," he said. I could hear the fear and anguish in his voice. My heart started to thud as I wondered what was going on.

"What's wrong?" I asked.

"It's Lily. She's gone missing Nash," Papa said.

"Shit. You've checked all her friends and stuff?" I asked.

"Yes. She went to school yesterday morning, but from what the school has said, she never made it."

I hummed, as suddenly my mind switched from son and brother to detective. It didn't matter that I had never met Lily, or that my Papa didn't speak to me much anymore. Right now, all that mattered was a girl was missing. I wouldn't have been so worried if it hadn't been for all the spate of kidnappings that we had been working on.

"Alright, you still live at the same house?" I asked

"Yes. Are you going to come, son?" Papa questioned, his voice sounded like a mix of unsure and pleading.

I wanted to growl at the use of the honorific. I hadn't been his son in a very long time. But none of that mattered. Lily didn't deserve my hurt feelings to get in the way of the investigation.

"Yes. I'll bring some of my teammates with me, we should be able to pick up on a scent and we can find her quickly. Hopefully, it is just a case of she decided to skip school and then stay out testing her boundaries," I said trying to soothe my father's panic.

"I hope so. Thank you, Nash."

"Alright, I'll see you soon," I said before ending the call. When I turned, I saw that the entire team was standing watching me with concern on their faces.

"That was my father. My little sister is twelve. She hasn't returned from school yesterday, Papa said that she never made it to school either."

Memphis nodded his head. "Alright, Nash, you, and Coltrane head over to your Papa's house. Bacchus and I will get to the school and question the teachers and headmaster. Raiden and Pax, you guys start traveling the routes that Lily is likely to take to school. Do you know where she would walk?"

I sighed. "I've never even met her before."

Memphis smiled warmly. "It's alright. She is another girl that has potentially been taken, we treat this case as such."

I nodded my head before looking over at Raiden and Pax. "If you guys come with us, Papa will be able to give you a list of her friends and the route she took to school."

"Can do," Raiden said.

We all got sorted and headed out the door. My stomach was rioting. In one sense I was glad that Papa called me, but it had been almost fifteen years since I'd seen him. I'd never even seen so much as a picture of Lily.

"We'll get through this man, and then we will debrief," Coltrane said as he gave my shoulder a squeeze.

I nodded my head and bit into my lip. I didn't know what was about to happen, but this had the potential of changing all my family's lives forever.

Chapter Seventeen

M y family home didn't look any different from the last time I'd been there. It would have been the last time I visited while at uni. Papa came and stood on the front porch as Coltrane pulled the van into the driveway. Apart from his greying hair, he looked just the same. He was still a strong moose shifter. His dark eyes looked panicked as he watched me get out of the car.

"Nash," he said with a breathy sigh. Tears were welled in his eyes as he opened his arms to me. Out of habit I stepped into my Papa's arms and allowed him to embrace me. "Thank you for coming."

"It's alright. These are my teammates. This is Coltrane, Raiden, and Pax. We need to ask some questions and get a list of all of Lily's friends and the route she took to school. Pax and Raiden will need to scent her so that they can follow her scent on the route she took," I explained.

Papa nodded his head and stepped back. "Yes, come in, I'll show you, her room."

We followed Papa into Lily's room. It was a typical teenage room. Pink and purples were splashed everywhere. Posters covered the walls and photos of her, and her friends filled in the gaps. I leaned forward to look at the pictures. The first time I'd even seen my little sister. Her dark hair and eyes were identical to mine.

"She is a fae?" Pax asked.

Papa nodded his head. "Yes. Her Mama is fae also."

"Are these pictures the most recent?" I asked.

Papa squinted at the photo where Lily was standing with her arm slung around the shoulders of a girl with bright red hair.

"Yes, that is her best friend Imogen," Papa answered.

"Can we get Imogen's address, and any other friends' names and addresses too please," Raiden asked.

"Yes, of course, my mate will know," Papa said as he turned from the room and left.

"Have you got her scent?" I asked.

Pax nodded his head. "Yep, there are only a few scents in here. There is the moose shifter of her father, fae of Lily and I assume her mother, but there is also a polar bear shifter, I'm thinking that is possibly one of her friends, and a pixie too."

"Nash," my stepmother, Stacey said as she came into the room.

"Stacey," I replied with a nod.

"Lucas said you need Lily's friend's names and addresses," she stated as she held out a piece of paper. I took it from her hand and looked down at the list. No names stood out but that didn't mean anything. I handed the list over to Raiden.

"Raiden and Pax are going to follow her scent to see if they can find where she went yesterday. The polar bear shifter and pixie are one of her friends?" I asked.

Stacey nodded. "Imogen is the pixie; her other friend Maisie is the polar bear shifter."

"And they were both at school today and yesterday?" I questioned.

"Yes, I spoke to them when Lily didn't come home. She hasn't just run away. She isn't like you," Stacey said with a sneer.

I looked over at her and raised an eyebrow. "This has nothing to do with me. I am here purely as a detective for the AJE authority. The problems that you and I have had, have no impact on this case."

"Right, of course, you wouldn't want to fix this problem. Instead, you are happy to see your Papa missing you."

I growled in my throat. "Enough. Do you want us to find Lily or not?"

"Of course, I fucking well do," Stacey spat.

"Good, then I suggest you drop the bullshit from our past and allow me and my team to do our fucking jobs."

Stacey's head snapped back as if I slapped her, and her cheeks tinted pink. I wasn't about to entertain her bullshit while there was a missing little girl.

"Alright, we will head out, I've got her scent. I'll ring you with more news when we know more," Pax said.

I nodded my head. "Thanks, man." I turned back to Stacey. "Right, let's go and sit and have a chat about Lily so that I can get a full understanding of what has likely happened. I need to know everything."

Stacey nodded her head but didn't say anything as she turned and left the bedroom, to walk into the kitchen where Papa was making cups of tea. Coltrane gave my shoulder a squeeze. It was good to know that I had my teammates who would have my back, as it seemed that Stacey wasn't going to let anything go. Not even while her daughter was missing.

Chapter Eighteen

M addox

We pulled into the lot where the new job was. "Shit this is eerie," Carl said as he looked out through the windscreen.

I nodded my head. The whole area had a weird feeling about it. I wasn't sure what it was. But it just felt spooky. Like the trees were watching us. The further into the lot we drove the less light that came in through the trees.

"They are going to have to clear a lot of the land first," Brandt noted.

"The clearing is just beyond these trees," I said as Carl continued along the narrow gravel road.

Finally, we emerged past the tree line into a clearing. It was going to only be large enough for the house to be built. I frowned as I wondered how the hell, we were going to be able to fit trucks down the driveway.

Carl pulled the van up and we emerged to investigate the clearing. I looked back at the narrow path. There was going to be no way that the trucks would be able to make it down that path. We would have to cut back the trees on the side of the path. That would push the price up.

Brandt, Carl, and I stood looking at the plans for the house on the front of the van and discussing which would be the optimal way of going about things.

"Hello," a soft voice said, causing all three of us to jump and spin around.

A woman that was sickly thin, stood behind us. Her grey hair hung limply around her shoulders. Her grey eyes were sharp. She looked like a witch that might feature in a fairy tale story, with her hook nose and dressed all in black. However, her scent told me that she was human.

"Where did you come from?" Carl asked with a growl in his voice.

A tinkle of laughter fell from her lips. "Sorry, I didn't mean to frighten you all. I walked. My husband is just parking the car."

"Are you Elizabeth?" I asked.

She smiled and nodded her head. "Yes. My husband Archie will be here in a moment. You must be Maddox."

"Yes. These are two members of my crew, Brandt, and Carl," I replied.

Elizabeth smiled at them and nodded her head. Out of nowhere, her husband came around the side of the van. The pair of them seemed to slink when they walked. It was eerie and add that to the terrifying surroundings, it made it all feel like we were stepping into a damned horror movie.

"So, what do you boys think?" Archie asked. In contrast to Elizabeth, he was tall with a dusting of ginger hair on his head. He had a thin wiry beard and his blue eyes looked like they were in a constant state of watering. When he walked it was done with a stiff stride, almost like he had a stick in his ass holding him straight.

"Well, we are going to need to cut back the trees on the path to the clearing, our supply trucks won't be able to get through," I explained.

Elizabeth gasped and looked up at Archie who shook his head. His frown deepened on his brow.

"No. That won't be possible," he said.

"Well, we aren't going to be able to carry the materials up the path by hand. That's just not possible," I argued.

Archie glared at me with his watery stare. His jaw tightened and I wondered briefly if he was going to hit me.

"I will have the trees sorted. You will start work next week?" he practically demanded.

I raised an eyebrow. "I can try to start as early as next week, however, that all depends on being able to get what you need by then. It is not a matter of just me and my crew working, we need to orchestrate with concreters and other trades."

Archie's brow pulled down further and his eyes narrowed into a glare. "You will start work next week," he growled through clenched teeth.

I folded my arms over my chest. Archie wasn't the first human I'd dealt with that thought he could boss me around because I was supernatural. Some humans saw the supernaturals as being beneath them. I never gave into bullies.

"As I said, we will try to start work next week. You are welcome to go through other builders, I can give you the number of others if you'd prefer?"

Archie blinked and looked briefly down at Elizabeth who was watching him with wide eyes.

He shook his head and cleared his throat. "That won't be necessary. I will have the trees trimmed back for trucks to make it into the clearing."

"Very well. I will gather my crew and I will give you a ring by the end of the week to tell you an exact day that we will be able to start work."

Archie nodded his head. I stuck my hand out to shake his, but he simply looked down at my hand before turning away and stalking down towards the path. Elizabeth gave me a tight smile and followed her husband, leaving Brandt, Carl, and me standing there watching after them.

"What the fuck was that?" Carl whispered.

"I don't know, but fucking creepy is an understatement," Brandt responded.

I nodded my head. My gut told me this was going to end up being a shitshow.

Chapter Nineteen

Nash

I sat at the kitchen table once Papa sat down with cups of tea for me and Coltrane. I held the picture of Lily in my hands. Papa's eyes were filled with tears, while Stacey continued to glare. If I didn't know that she was Lily's mother, I would be questioning it. I felt like she didn't really care about the fact that her daughter was missing, she was more pissed about the fact that I was there. Her priorities were fucked up. But I guess that was why we never saw eye to eye.

"Papa, can you tell me about Lily's last few days?" I asked gently.

Papa looked up at me and nodded his head. "She was a typical twelve-year-old. She is headstrong and we would have our odd blow-up, but nothing that would make her run off."

"She didn't run away," Stacey spat. "Only one of your children did that."

"Enough, Stacey," Papa growled. "Now is not the time."

Stacey blew out a breath and folded her arms across her chest. "I promise you Stacey, once Lily is found, you can do all your yelling and growling at me you like. But right now, our main concern is Lily."

Stacey rolled her eyes. I sighed, it wasn't going to matter what I said, she just didn't like me. Not that I'd ever done anything to her. But it is what it is.

"Did you have any arguments with Lily over the last few days?" Coltrane asked.

"No, she'd been happy the last few days. She was getting ready to go camping with Russell and his mate," Papa answered.

"Did you notice her talking about anyone new? Someone that you hadn't met before?"

Papa hummed and shook his head, before looking at Stacey. "Stace?"

Stacey shook her head. "No."

"Does she use social media?" I asked.

"Yeah, she has a Facebook," Stacey replied.

"Do you know the login details?" Coltrane asked. "If we can look at her Facebook then we will be able to make sure she wasn't talking to someone that could be a danger to her."

Stacey nodded her head and stood going to her phone that was sitting on the kitchen bench. She pressed into the screen before turning it. Lily's profile was loaded. I took the phone from Stacey and laid it between Coltrane and me. Coltrane pressed on the screen to open the messenger. We glanced through the messages. There was a message between her and Imogen. A group chat for her and a group of kids that appeared to be school friends, but nothing that seemed out of place.

Coltrane went to the archived messages, but once again it didn't show anything. I skimmed through the message between her and Imogen, but nothing stood out. It was all typical teenage chatter.

As I skimmed through the messages one name kept coming up. "Who is Bryce?" I asked.

"That's Imogen's older brother," Papa replied.

"Okay, we should get Raiden and Pax to talk to him too. It seems that Lily had a crush on him, she talks a lot about Bryce," I said to Coltrane who quickly sent a message to Pax.

"Yeah, she did, but he is a lot older, he isn't interested in Lily," Stacey said with a sigh.

I nodded my head. "It's good to cover all bases, just in case."

"There is nothing else in her social media?" Papa asked.

I shook my head. "No. She is talking to her friends like a normal teenage girl. Have you noticed any cars or people hanging around the house or perhaps following you when you are with Lily. Anyone that stands out as a little strange?"

Papa sat back in his seat and hummed. Stacey for the first time since I came in the house looked worried. Like suddenly it hit her that her daughter could have been abducted and in real trouble.

"That man we saw in the supermarket," Stacey suddenly said. Papa's eyes flared and he nodded his head.

"Tell me about it," I replied.

"We went to the supermarket to get some food; Lily was with us. Every aisle we went down there was a man there, the same man. At first, I didn't take any notice, I just thought it was a weird co-incidence. Then Lily asked if she could get some sweets, so I said yes, and she went to the candy aisle. When she hadn't come back, I went to find her. She was standing in the candy aisle talking to the man. I walked up to her, and the man quickly said goodbye and left. I asked Lily what he wanted, and she said he was asking her questions about the local schools and things for kids to do in Lalbert," Stacey explained.

I exchanged a look with Coltrane, and he nodded his head before typing out a message in his phone to Raiden and Pax. We would go to the supermarket and hopefully they would have CCTV of the man.

"When was this?" I asked

"Um was it Thursday?" Stacey asked Papa.

"Yes, Thursday, we were there about six," Papa answered.

Coltrane stood from the table. "I'll ring the supermarket and see if they have CCTV and get them to pull it."

"Did he say his name to Lily?" I asked.

Stacey shook her head. "I don't know. I didn't ask. I just thought he was a weirdo and didn't think more about it. Do you think that he was stalking Lily?"

"I don't know for sure. You might be right, he might just be some weirdo, but it seems a strange co-incidence."

My phone buzzed and when I looked down at the screen, I saw that it was a message from Pax. *We've got her scent. It ends literally at the edge of the school.*

"Pax and Raiden have her scent. It seems that she has been taken just as she reached school," I explained to Papa and Stacey. Papa let out a groan and ran his hands up over his face.

My phone buzzed again. *Scout is here, she was dragged unwillingly into a car. They have a lead on her.*

"We have got a member of the Onyx Rebels out there with Pax and Raiden. They are a raven shifter with immense power, they have got a lead on her. We will do everything we can to get her back," I said as I reached out and took Papa's hand in mine. Gods I hoped we were able to get her back.

"Thank you, son," Papa said.

I nodded my head and stood from the table before going out to find Coltrane who was on the phone to the supermarket still. Once he ended the call, he looked up at me.

"The manager is pulling the footage for us, we can go over there now," he said.

I quickly explained the messages that I got from Pax.

Coltrane nodded his head. "Good. If we can get the footage from the supermarket, we will be able to compare it with Scout and see if we are looking at the same guy."

My phone rang again and when I looked at the ID, I saw that it was Kade calling. "Kade," I answered.

"Nash. I'm sending Arcadia out to you guys to watch the footage; she is going to be working with Scout and Kaki. We are going to find your sister."

"Thank you, Kade," I said as I cleared my throat. I closed my eyes and sent out a prayer to the creator. Please let her be safe.

Chapter Twenty

M addox

By the time we got back to the workshop, I'd managed to shake off the creeps that Archie and Elizabeth gave me. Our ride back was done in silence as we all thought over everything. I'd called my concreter and plumber and organized for them to be able to start late next week. I hated giving into Archie's demands, but unfortunately, I couldn't always choose my client's attitudes.

The rest of the day was spent orchestrating my crews on the jobs, I'd gone out to check on my guys and was ribbed over and over about now being a mated man. I lapped it all up. I loved that I was now mated. I couldn't be prouder.

Just before five, my phone rang and when I looked, I saw that it was Nash's number. "Hey baby," he said once I answered.

"Hey, you sound exhausted," I said.

"I am stressed that's for sure. I'm not going to be able to get back to you tonight. My sister Lily, has been abducted. I'm working flat out trying to find her," Nash explained.

"Shit, what do you need me to do?" I asked.

"Nothing baby. There isn't anything you can do. Just look after yourself. I'm going to try and be home tomorrow."

"It's alright, I completely understand, don't stress about me. Just focus on finding your sister. Do you have any leads?"

"Yeah, we know she has been abducted by at least one human guy. We just must try and find her. Kade is putting out a media release tonight about it."

"I'll watch the news and get my crews to keep their eyes out for him."

"Thank you, baby," Nash replied.

We didn't talk for long as he had to get back to work. My heart ached. I knew that Nash didn't have anything to do with his family and in one sense I hoped that this was an event to at least open a line of communication. But I worried and hoped that they found Lily before she was hurt.

I knew that there were abductions of supernatural children all over Lalbert. Sadly, Morpheus was responsible for many of those abductions. Since they were disbanded though, the public was left to assume that the abductions were happening less. If it hadn't been for my friendship with Anghus and the Devil's Advocates, then I wouldn't know about how many were still happening.

I guessed it was something I was going to have to get used to hearing about, especially now that I was mated to an AJE authority detective. It tore at my heart though. I could have been one of those kids. I was lucky that Tom and Margaret took me in. I imagine if I had been left to be homeless then I would have possibly been taken and made to be bred. I shuddered at the thought.

I pressed on Tom's contact in my phone and brought the phone to my ear.

"Hello Son," Tom answered with a smile in his voice.

"Tom," I said with a smile. I always loved it when he called me son, it meant so much to me.

"How have you been?"

"Not bad, I was sick last week, just some sort of tummy bug."

"You should have rung, you know that Margaret would have been around with her soup for you," Tom scolded.

I smiled. Margaret, no matter how old we got, always made chicken noodle soup whenever we were sick. She was what a true mother was. She loved with her whole heart, and no one was treated any differently.

"I was alright, I was looked after," I said.

"Oh? Is there something you need to tell me, Maddox?" Tom asked with laughter in his voice.

I chuckled. "Yeah, there is. I met my mate."

Tom called out to Margaret, and I could hear her in the background. Margaret let out a whoop.

"Who is your mate, Maddox?" Margaret asked as Tom obviously put the phone on speaker.

"His name is Nash. He is a moose shifter. A detective for the AJE authority, shifter unit.

"Oh, that is wonderful. You will have to bring him around. I want to meet him. And you know that Allison and Alexander will want to meet him too, Alexander will need to interrogate him."

I laughed. Alexander was a human cop. There was a probable chance that Alexander already knew Nash. It was something that I never thought to ask Nash.

"We will come around. Nash is busy working on an abduction now. His little sister was abducted yesterday."

"Oh no, that's awful. I saw something about it on the news," Tom said.

"Yeah, I said I'd watch the news to see if I've seen the guy that took her."

"Kade Sinclair was giving a press conference, he said that she was taken by a human. I wondered if it was that horrible group Morpheus. I'd heard rumors that they were trying to start up again," Tom continued.

"I hope not."

"Me too. I remember Nash's younger brother, Russell, who was in my woodwork class before I retired. Lily is too young to have been at school when I was still teaching."

"Nash doesn't talk to his family. Apparently, his step mum caused a lot of issues," I explained.

"That's a shame. Hopefully, they can put everything aside so that they can work together for Lily's sake. Even if they find her, her healing will take time. She will need her family around her."

"I agree," I said with a sigh. I knew just how important family was. Even if they weren't blood-related. We all needed family.

Chapter Twenty-One

Nash

After explaining to Papa and Stacey that Kade was going to be coming out to do a press conference and the information that Scout had, Coltrane and I headed over to meet the rest of the team at the school.

"Alright, I've got stills from the CCTV footage at the supermarket," Pax said.

"Good, I've got CCTV footage from the front of the school. There was a suspicious car driving up and down the street, in one shot you can see the driver, so I want to compare shots," Memphis said.

Pax nodded and opened the folder to show a man with a balding head and a ratty beard if that was what you could even call a beard.

"That's the same guy," Memphis said as he opened his own folder to show the photo he had of the guy in the car. The photo that Memphis held was blurry, but there was no mistaking that the guy in the car was the same one as the supermarket.

"Were you able to get registration details on the car?" I asked.

Memphis shook his head. "No tags. And the car is a common Mazda. It's going to be hard to find him."

Scout and Arcadia joined our group. Pax passed the photo over to Scout who nodded their head. "Same guy. He's the one that took Lily."

"Any idea on who he is?" I asked.

Scout and Arcadia shared a look. "All I know now is that he is human. Lily was taken from the edge of the school grounds, over there," Scout said as they pointed in the direction that Lily was abducted from.

"There was a struggle. She fought hard, I could see that Lily recognized the guy, but she didn't know his name or anything. From what I was able to see she screamed and fought. The man is traveling with another woman. They are new to the area, but looking to set down roots here," Arcadia explained.

I nodded my head. "Alright, so now we just have to find where he took her to."

"I have a general idea. The man wasn't closed off. I don't believe he is working for Morpheus, but I could be wrong on that. However, I could see what he was thinking about and the direction that he was planning to take her," Scout explained.

"Alright, let's get ready, Kade has said that as soon as we have a location, he will have the vampire team on standby ready to go. Merza has witches, Kaylee and the medics are on call. Scout, I believe that the Onyx Rebels are also ready to go in?" Memphis said.

Scout nodded their head. "Hawke, Kaki, and Jabari are all on standby. Nova will shift with Jabari and fly overhead."

"Alright, that's good. Arcadia you come with me and lead us to where you believe that Lily is being held. We will stop short of the place, so as not to spook anyone," Memphis directed.

With that, we piled into the vans. I sat behind Memphis who was driving with Arcadia in the passenger seat beside him. Next to me was Pax, while the others went in the other van. Arcadia started to direct Memphis out towards Winchester, which ran along the eastern border of Lalbert. Separating the two was thick pockets of forest. It would be easy for anyone to hide or get lost in the area. Not many people lived in the forest because there wasn't enough light, it was dark and gloomy. Many shifters used the forest as running grounds.

"Alright, pull up when you can," Arcadia said. "I need to get out and get my bearings, but we are close."

Memphis pulled into a small cut-off in the road and Arcadia stepped out of the car. Coltrane who was driving the other van pulled in behind us. By the time I got out of the van, Scout was walking towards Arcadia. We stood quietly as the pair placed their hands on the trees surrounding the area and closed their eyes.

Arcadia and Scout opened their eyes in complete synchronicity, which was eerie, and nodded their heads. When they came towards us, I knew they had a location.

"Alright, I can see where the man was thinking of," Scout said. "However, this isn't going to be an easy rescue."

I winced at the sound of that. "How so?" Memphis asked.

"The place is booby-trapped. They are armed to the hilt and ready to take on an army," Arcadia answered.

"Shit. Alright, this isn't going to be moved on quickly. We need to plan. Kade is giving the press conference and hopefully, that will spook them out of hiding. I'll organize for the vampire team to surround the place. If we can have Hawke, Scout, Nova, and Jabari in the canopies watching the property that would be good. I don't want to send anyone in on foot, if it is booby-trapped there is likely that there are things set up to kill us."

Scout nodded their head. "There are. The only way that we could safely approach the house is via the driveway, which is a narrow lane-like path. They will not only hear us coming but I believe they will see us too. There are cameras everywhere."

"Yeah, okay, that's no good. Shit. Alright, we need eyes in the sky, Scout can you organize that, and give us as much information as possible. I'll set the vampires up surrounding the forest area but staying on main roads. If they emerge from the property, they will be seen and stopped," Memphis instructed.

"Should we get the Devil's involved?" Bacchus asked.

"Yeah, might be a good idea. Let's have them on standby so that if this guy leaves with Lily, then they can be back up for the vampires."

"Alright on it," Bacchus said as he lifted his phone to his ear and walked away.

"How far away is the place?" Memphis asked Arcadia.

She turned her phone that had a map open. The property was only a kilometer up the road. It was well hidden, and you could barely even see it with the satellite photo.

"They are hidden," Memphis said.

"Yep. This isn't their first rodeo," Scout replied.

"Do you think there are other children in there?" I asked.

Scout twisted their lips and shrugged their shoulders. "I can see other children, but as to whether they are still with these people or not, I don't know for sure."

"We will prepare for there being extras," Memphis replied. "Alright let's get back to the precinct and plan this out properly."

I didn't like the idea of leaving without Lily. But I had to be logical we couldn't just rush in and potentially not only have Lily injured and killed but also lose members of our teams. That wasn't something I was willing to risk. The more we planned the less danger we were likely to face.

Chapter Twenty-Two

M addox

Once I got off the phone with Tom and Margaret, I turned the television on and searched through the channels looking for footage about Lily's abduction. Every channel had scrolling banners about the kidnapping but nothing that showed a picture of the abductors. I paused once I reached the news channel and sat back on the couch waiting for the story to come back up.

"We come back to our breaking news and amber alert," the news broadcaster said. The camera was focused on the woman's face as she spoke. "The AJE authority is asking for help from the public in finding Lily Andrews. She was last seen walking to Lalbert High School on Jenner Road. It was here that she was abducted by a man, driving a red Mazda. Any witnesses are urged to contact Kade Sinclair at the AJE Authority."

"Show the picture of the guy," I said with a frown.

The broadcaster flicked off to a stock photo of the car, but they didn't show the man. I shook my head. *Why wouldn't they show the picture?* I picked up my phone and opened the messages. *Why aren't the news programs showing the guy that took Lily?* I sent Nash.

His response was almost instant. *Kade decided not to show the picture of the guy. He wants to hold back.*

That didn't make any sense to me. In my mind, if more people knew what he looked like, the easier it would be to catch him. But I had to trust that Kade and the AJE authority had a reason.

We have a potential address for her. We are going in tonight. Nash messaged again.

Please be careful. I need you back here with me at the end of it all. I replied.

I'll be there baby, no fear of that.

I smiled at my phone and sent a love heart emoji. It was amazing to think that I'd only known Nash for not even a week, yet my heart longed for him in a way that I'd never felt before. I sighed and flicked the television off and closed my eyes.

My phone began to ring causing me to jump. I looked down at the phone to see Carl's number coming up.

"Hey man," I answered.

"Maddox, do you reckon that those people that we went to see today, have anything to do with that little girl's abduction?"

I hummed. "Na. I mean they were creepy that was for sure. But they were old and frail. I don't reckon it was them."

Carl sighed. "I wish they'd show a picture of the people."

"Yeah, I just asked Nash why they weren't. Apparently, Kade Sinclair wanted to hold back the photo."

"So, they know who took her?"

"They know what the guy looks like, I don't know that they know who he is yet," I replied, not sure how much information I should give away. I didn't know if Nash was supposed to tell me that they had found an address for the man that took Lily.

"Shit, I hope they get him. I feel sick over the thought of that little girl," Carl said.

Carl was mated with a tribe of kids of his own. He had like thirteen kids at last count. All hyena shifters. It was always loud and busy whenever I went over to their house. It was great, the kids were adorable, but I always came away exhausted. I didn't know how Carl's mate, Shelley ever managed to cope.

"It's horrible. The girl is Nash's sister," I said.

"Oh fuck. I'm sorry man. I didn't know."

"It's alright. Nash had never met her. His family is as dysfunctional as mine," I chuckled.

"Woah, is that even possible?"

I barked out a laugh. Yeah, it wasn't that realistic. All my crew knew Tom and Margaret, but they also knew that Tom and Margaret weren't my biological parents. The fact that they were humans gave that away. I hadn't really talked in depth about my parents to my employees, but they knew that I didn't speak to them, and knew that my father was an abusive asshole.

It was only Carter and Nash that knew about how bad it was growing up in the Chan household. Thankfully I was out, and I knew that I would raise my children in a much different way. For one they wouldn't know what it was like to be beaten or fear me or Nash. That just wasn't going to ever happen.

Chapter Twenty-Three

Nash

"We've got Scout, Nova, Jabari, and Hawke in the air watching over the house," Kade said as he stood in the front of the shifter unit. The room was crowded with shifters, vampires, and detectives from AJE Authority as well as members of the Devil's Advocates and Onyx Rebels.

"What do we know about them so far?" Merza asked.

"We have been able to get a name, I'll turn it over to Alexander for the information that they've found out," Kade said, before turning to a guy that I recognized from the human department of the precinct.

"Thanks, Kade. We were able to run the photo that you guys got from the supermarket through the database as well as the make of his car. His name is Archibald Rose. Born in 1948. His registered address is in Sydney. The house that you believe that Lily is being held in is rented by who we believe is Archibald's wife, Elizabeth Rose. She was born in 1946. But that is all we were able to find out about her. My team is still delving into records in hope that we can discover more."

"Do either of them have a criminal history?" Bacchus questioned.

Alexander shook his head. "There was one arrest for Archibald back in 1968 for an assault charge against a co-worker in Sydney. But that is it."

I winced; it didn't sound like we had much at all to go on. "Thank you, Alexander. The human teams are working alongside us on this one to get as much information as possible," Kade said.

Alexander nodded his head and smiled. He glanced around the room and caught my eye before smirking. I wasn't sure what that meant but I tipped my head and gave him a smile.

Coltrane elbowed me in the side. "You've no idea who that is, do you?" I glanced at Coltrane and shook my head making him chuckle. "That's your brother-in-law. Maddox's adopted brother."

"Oh shit, really?" I said glancing over at Alexander who was busy talking quietly to Merza. I was going to have to go and introduce myself. I had no idea that Maddox's brother was a cop. I wondered why he hadn't mentioned it. Not that we had a lot of time to talk between him being sick and then our mating.

"Okay," Kade said as he brought the map of the property up on the screen at the front of the room. "Scout has been keeping us updated with information. There has been no sight of Archibald or Elizabeth in the time that they have been there. No one has entered or left the house. Scout was able to land in the driveway and see that the red Mazda is parked in a carport next to the house. They said that they were able to hear crying, who we believe is Lily. Her cries have been ignored. Scout believes that they have her in perhaps a basement, although it is a one-level house, to Scout it sounded like the cries were coming from somewhere within the house."

"While Scout was canvasing the house, Nova and Hawke were able to survey the land surrounding the property. Behind the main house is a large tin building. It has no windows and only one door in. Nova believed that she could hear voices coming from within the building but wasn't able to decipher if those sounds were coming from other omegas, or if it were Archibald and Elizabeth. Without going in we wouldn't be able to tell."

"We need a small shifter," Pax said.

"What about my brother-in-law March, he is a spider shifter and Israel is redcap so he can alter into anything?" Bacchus asked.

"Don't send March in, I'm not comfortable with that," Israel said. "I can get in and out unseen."

"Okay, that sounds like an idea. Israel, I want you to take some back up with you also though, I'm not comfortable you going in on your own," Kade said.

"I'll go with him," Raiden said.

"What about the traps?" Coltrane questioned.

"Nova was able to spot traps, they are placed around the ground, some are spikes buried into the ground, others are bear traps and rabbit traps hidden amongst the foliage. However, there is a pebbled path that leads from the house to the garage. My suggestion would be for Israel to shift into whichever alter you plan to shift to and then be carried in by either Scout or Hawke. I think Nova and Jabari will be too noticeable if they land in there."

Israel nodded his head. "I think Scout will be better. If they drop me onto the roof of the tin building, I'll be able to find an entrance. I should also be able to find an entrance into the house to see where exactly Lily is and what condition she is in."

"Perfect," Kade said as his eyes shifted and glazed over. Within seconds his vision snapped back to normal, and he smiled at Israel. "Scout is waiting for you. Take the bike, but park in the reserve at the end of the road. Scout will meet you then and take you from there."

Israel nodded and turned, slapping Anghus's hand as he left.

Chapter Twenty-Four

B y the time it was nearing midnight Israel was back at the precinct with the information he was able to gather. Scout had been in constant contact and from what they could see no one had left or entered either building since our discovery of them. I wasn't sure if this was a good or bad sign.

"Alright Israel, what have you got?" Kade asked.

Israel pulled up the map of the house onto the big screen. "The place is sealed tight, it was hard going to get in. There were no gaps or openings on the roof or around the walls. Even the door is completely sealed from the inside, blocking all the gaps."

"How are they getting air in there?" Jai asked.

Israel shrugged his shoulders. "I couldn't work that out. But I could hear voices in there from the outside. I went to the back of the building and tried digging under as a rabbit alter, but the tin is literally buried into the ground about three feet. I was finally able to shrink down small enough, and I'm talking silk worm size, to get through a tiny gap between the ground and the tin. They don't want people in or out of that building."

"So, when you got in, what were you able to find?" Kade pressed.

"I shifted into a fly so that I would be less obvious, but the building is completely dark. There appear to be cages running the entire length of the building on either side, with just a narrow aisle down the middle. I would think there are around about twelve to thirteen boys and girls, ranging from the ages of seven to around early twenties in there. They are all extremely thin, filthy, the stench of the place is gut-churning."

"Shit," I growled. "Were they being bred?"

Israel shook his head. "None of them were pregnant. I couldn't tell what the reason was for them being kept in the cages, but they weren't pregnant."

"What kind of supernaturals are we talking about?" Memphis asked.

"Mostly fae. There were a couple of shifters, but amongst the stench of waste and dirt, it was hard to be able to decipher exactly what they were, and even with the night vision of a fly I couldn't see them completely."

"Alright, so the house?" Kade asked.

"The house was a lot easier to get into. At first, I couldn't see where they had Lily. I could hear crying, but I couldn't work out where it was coming from. Archibald and Elizabeth don't appear to be husband and wife, they have separate rooms. Elizabeth is old, like ancient. Her room is this one at the back," Israel said as he pointed at the screen to the back of the house. "Then Archibald's is here at the front of the house. There didn't appear to be any other rooms, that's what had me so confused. The crying sounded like it was all around like it was seeping through the walls. I couldn't work it out. But then I noticed the speakers. The sick cunt's have a speaker system set up throughout the whole house playing on repeat the sounds of crying."

"Does that mean that you weren't able to find Lily?" I asked.

Israel sighed and looked over at me. He nodded his head. "I'm sorry. But I just couldn't find where she was. I literally scoured the entire house. That doesn't mean that she's not one of the people in that shed. But I've literally gone over the whole house. That's what took me so long, I was searching everywhere."

I sighed feeling completely defeated. There was hope that Lily was in the shed with the other kids, but if she wasn't it made me sick to think about where she could be.

"So, what do we do?" Memphis asked.

"Scout, Nova, Hawke, and Jabari have gone over the entire property, they've been able to source out all the booby traps and mark them with magic so that we can see them. Kaki and Arcadia have placed wards over the house so that Archibald and Elizabeth won't be able to exit the building. Did you notice weapons?" Kade asked Israel.

Israel nodded his head. "Yep, there are guns. Kept in Archibald's room. I can disable them before you guys go in."

"Excellent, do that," Kade replied before looking at his watch. "It is midnight now. I think we should head in now. We can at least arrest Archibald and Elizabeth and question them. We will release the kids in the shed and hope that Lily is among them, if she isn't then we will interrogate the humans and hopefully get our answers."

I didn't like the idea that we were going to expect answers from Archibald and Elizabeth. Something told me they weren't going to give up any knowledge. I just hoped that Lily was in the shed and not being kept somewhere else. We literally didn't know anything about Archibald and Elizabeth, we didn't know how deep their operation went or who they were working with. For all we knew, they were working directly with Ettore and that could mean that Lily was already in the underworld.

Chapter Twenty-Five

Maddox

I didn't sleep a wink throughout the night. My mind was filled with worry about Lily and Nash. I hadn't heard from him and didn't want to text or ring him, I didn't want to interrupt the important work he was doing. I'd left the news program running in hope that they might decide to show the face of Lily's abductor. There was no new information, only that Lily had been taken from her school.

I'd dragged myself out to the workshop just before eight. Even though I just wanted to curl up in bed and sleep for the day, I had work to do. I had to make sure my crews were doing everything they needed, and I still needed to work out some things with supplies for Archie and Elizabeth's home.

I scrubbed my hands up over my face and flopped into the seat in my office. The door to the workshop opened and when I looked up my heart skipped a beat as Nash came through.

"Hey baby," he said quietly.

"Any news?" I asked.

He sighed and shrugged his shoulders. "We raided on the place last night, there were twelve kids there, but Lily wasn't among them."

"Shit. So, they have abducted others?" I questioned.

Nash nodded. "Yeah. We don't even know where these kids came from. The youngest is six. The eldest was twenty-two and she doesn't even remember where she came from. She only remembers being with Archibald and Elizabeth."

I gasped and my eyes widened. "Wait. Archie and Elizabeth Rose?" I asked.

Nash frowned and nodded his head. "Do you know them?"

"Yeah. They wanted me to start building them a house next week."

Nash's eyes widened. "Shit. We didn't know they had other properties."

"This place is on Tomlinson Road," I said as I pulled out the information that I had for Archie and Elizabeth. There is no way that it is a co-incidence. None of us had heard of them, they were new to Lalbert, it had to be the same people.

Nash turned his phone to face me, and I saw a picture of the man who was the same man I'd met the day before.

"Yeah, that's him. I met him and Elizabeth yesterday with Brandt and Carl."

Nash swiped his thumb over the screen of his phone and a woman's face appeared. It was Elizabeth. I nodded my head. "That's her."

"Alright," Nash said as he leaned down and pressed a kiss on my lips. "Thank you, baby, you might have just opened this case."

I smiled but shook my head. "There weren't any buildings on that land though. It was surrounded by woods, and then a clearing beyond the trees."

Nash twisted his lips to the side. "Can you come into the precinct with me? Maybe bring Brandt and Carl too?"

"Yeah, I can do that," I said as I pulled my phone out of my pocket and pressed on Carl's number, he wasn't due in for another hour.

"Hey Boss," Carl answered.

"Carl, you were right about Archie and Elizabeth. Nash is here, it was them. Can you meet me with Brandt at the AJE precinct?"

"Holy Shit, I knew there was something fucking off about them. Yeah, I'll ring Brandt now and we will meet you there."

"Thanks, man," I replied before ending the call. "They are going to meet us there."

"Awesome. I've messaged Kade to let him know what you've just told me," Nash said before he stopped and cocked his head to the side to look at me. "Did you sleep last night?"

I sighed and shook my head. "No. I was worried about you and Lily."

Nash's frown deepened. "I don't want you to worry about me."

"I can't help it. You're my mate. I'm going to worry."

"I guess that's true. But I don't want you to miss out on sleep. It's not good for you. I don't want you to get sick. Especially if you are pregnant."

I smiled and stroked a hand over my belly. "I really hope I am."

Nash's smile was dynamic as he looked down at me. "I hope so too. Let's get through this and then we will find out and celebrate."

I grinned and nodded my head. Nash took my hand and pulled me up out of the chair and led me towards the door of the workshop. I quickly locked up and followed Nash to the car. I hoped that mine, Carl's, and Brandt's information would help to find Lily.

Chapter Twenty-Six

Nash

This was huge. The fact that Archibald and Elizabeth had another property was complete news to us. I'd sat in on the first round of interviews that Alexander had conducted with Archibald, but he wasn't giving up anything. Never in a million years would I have thought that Maddox might know who our kidnappers were.

The conditions were far worse than we could ever have begun to imagine. The smell was the most putrid thing I'd ever been witness to. The children, well mostly children were another story altogether. I still didn't quite comprehend what the hell I'd been looking at. When we pulled them from their cages, they were practically feral.

One of the children had even bitten Coltrane as he tried to bring her out of the cage. It was something out of a horror show. And when we got them into the light of the property it became more like a freak show. These children, they weren't just omegas. They weren't just abused. They had been tortured. All of them were blind, having had their eyes literally removed.

Their bodies had been carved, some were missing limbs, while others had extra limbs that had been sewn to them. I'd never seen anything like it. My stomach was still churning at the memory of what I'd seen. Each child was able to speak, although the younger ones' vocabulary was limited. I had no idea what Archibald and Elizabeth were doing to them. Or what kind of science experiment they were trying to create, but it was horrific.

Kaylee and the other medics had taken one look at the kids and were speechless. I'd noticed tears in the eyes of several seasoned detectives. I didn't blame them. My heart ached. My stomach felt ill. We didn't even scratch the surface of what the kids had potentially been through and the thought that Lily was possibly hurt or going to be hurt sickened me.

I'd spoken to Papa after the raid and broke the news to him that Lily wasn't among the kids. I told him that I wasn't about to give up. But inside my gut kept telling me that this was going to be bad. The child they had wasn't going to be the same child they got back.

"Hey, you never told me that Alexander, was a cop," I said to Maddox as I pulled into the precinct.

Maddox smiled and shrugged. "I forgot," he laughed. "Well not that I forgot he was a cop, I just for some reason didn't put AJE authority and police together."

I grinned. "He seems like a nice guy. He is working with us on this investigation. I didn't even know who he was, it was Coltrane that pointed him out."

Maddox laughed. "He is easy going. A bit of a joker, so expect to be pranked at some stage. That is his welcome to the family."

I smiled. Family. That word had started to take on all new meaning to me recently. On one hand, I had my friends, and now my mate who I saw as family. But after spending time with Papa and seeing that he seemed to want to mend broken fences, I wondered if there might be a chance to overcome the pain that I'd felt and forgive everyone. Maybe there was a chance to have my biological family. Stacey still hated me, and I wondered if that was going to be something I could simply overlook. Time would tell.

When we entered the shifter unit room, everyone was crowded around, obviously waiting. I noticed that Alexander was watching the door. A smile crept across his face as he saw Maddox enter in behind me. Alexander made a beeline for us and opened his arms to Maddox, who immediately enveloped his brother in a tight hug.

"Maddox. Dad told me that you had found a mate, fancy that mate being one of my workmates," Alexander said with a grin as he looked at Maddox's face.

"I'm really happy," Maddox replied.

"Good," Alexander answered before turning to me. "I didn't get to formally meet you yesterday with everything going on. Nash, it is great to have you as a brother and I trust that you will take great care of Maddox."

I smiled and reached out a hand to shake with Alexander's. "With my life."

"That's what I like to hear," he replied turning back to Maddox. "So, I hear that you had the misfortune of meeting our pieces of shit."

Maddox wrinkled his nose and nodded his head. "Yeah, creepy bastards."

"You can say that again," Alexander replied with a chuckle.

"Brandt and Carl were with me, they said they were going to meet me here," Maddox said just as two men entered.

"Right on cue," Alexander laughed as he went to greet the two men, I assumed were Carl and Brandt.

"Thank you for coming in Maddox, this will be very helpful," Kade said as he stepped towards us.

"You're welcome. I'm hoping that our help can find Lily. I feel sick over this."

Kade nodded his head. "Any bit of information will be greatly accepted right now."

Chapter Twenty-Seven

Maddox

Kade took Carl, Brandt, and me into an interview room with Nash and Alexander. I felt comfortable telling them everything we knew. I wanted to find Lily just as much as the others did.

"Thank you for coming in, this is a bit of a nightmare, I'm afraid," Kade started.

"If we can help then I'm happy to do so," Carl replied.

"Can you tell me everything you know about the block of land?" Kade asked.

"Of course," I said glancing at Carl and Brandt. "It is surrounded by woods. We had to ask Archie to cut back the trees so that we would be able to get trucks down the path to the clearing."

"Yeah, he was pissed about having to do it. We just thought he was weird, but it makes me wonder if there is something in the tree's that he is hiding," Carl said.

"You didn't see any buildings?" Kade asked.

"No. The trees are so thick along the path, that most of the light is literally blocked out. It was impossible to see through them. We followed the path until we reached the clearing and then stopped. But one weird thing was the way Elizabeth and Archie entered," Brandt said.

"Oh yeah," I replied and looked up at Kade. "They didn't drive in as we did. They said that they parked on the road and walked in. But when we left, we never saw any cars parked out on the road."

Carl and Brandt nodded. "I saw the direction that Archie came from, but it wasn't from the path either, he seemed to come out of the woods beside the path," Carl said.

"That's interesting," Kade replied. "I'm going to get Scout, Nova, Hawke, and Jabari to do a flyover. If they booby-trapped the house, I'm suspecting they will do the same for this block."

"There were no traps on the path or in the clearing that we could easily see," I said.

Kade nodded his head as he typed out a message on his phone. "Yeah, I suspect if they were going to trap the area, they would do it in the woods. Alexander, can you pull up a satellite image of the property, we might be able to see if there are any other buildings amongst the woods."

Alexander typed into the computer in front of him and a screen flicked on behind where Kade was sitting. Suddenly there was a picture looking down at the earth over the property.

"Are you able to pinpoint where the path is?" Kade asked.

"Yeah, I can," Carl said as he stood and went to the screen. "It starts here and then winds through; you can see a slight gap in the tree line. That's the path, which then leads to this clearing. I had a look last night on the satellite because I wanted to see where we could set up amenities while we were working, and there seems to be a path on this side too."

Carl traced his finger along with the screen where I could see there was a small break in the trees. Without taking great notice it would be something that would be easy to miss.

"Scan around Alexander and zoom in slightly, let's see if we can possibly see anything that is a building," Kade directed.

Alexander moved the photo around and zoomed in enough that it made everything a little closer. All of us stared at the screen. I chewed on my lip as I scanned the area.

"Where in the woods did you see Archie come into the clearing from?" I asked Carl.

He tapped on the screen in the direction that he saw Archie entering the clearing. It wasn't right next to the path but at least ten to twelve feet away.

"Wait, try and zoom in where he came in from," Carl said. Alexander moved the image and zoomed in. "There. Just left to your mouse pointer."

I leaned forward trying to work out what I was looking for that Carl had spotted. Alexander moved the image over a little more and zoomed in a small amount. Suddenly it became clear, another path, this one nothing more than a walking path, but as we followed it, there was a slight reflection hitting the screen.

"A building," Kade said. "Good spotting." He picked up his phone off the table and brought it to his ear. "Scout, we have a building, when flying overhead it is just east to the driveway. It looks like they've tried to camouflage it. We are going to drive out there and meet you. Gather as much information as you can."

Ending the call, Kade stood from his seat. "Thank you so much, guys, for coming in and for your help. I appreciate it."

I smiled and stood, glancing over at Nash who smiled tenderly at me. He bent forward and kissed me briefly on the lips. "Go home and get some sleep baby. I'll give you a call once we've raided this place."

I nodded my head and gave him a smile. "I will."

Kade, Alexander, and Nash left the room, leaving behind, me, Brandt, and Carl. "Fuck I hope they find that little girl," Brandt said.

I nodded my head. "Me too."

Chapter Twenty-Eight

Nash

I left Maddox with another quick kiss on the lips before following Kade and the rest of the teams out to the vans. Kade had been able to speak to Scout before we left and we learned that this property also was booby-trapped with spikes buried into the ground amongst the forested areas, however, the paths were empty.

From what Scout could tell there were people at the property. They were able to hear crying and a few voices talking. We were going in pretty much blind which made me nervous. Kade had organized with the Devil's Advocates to meet us at the property, they would send Israel in first.

The human team had stayed behind and would continue to interrogate Archibald and Elizabeth further. We didn't expect a lot of information from them. They were pretty much refusing to say anything. We had plenty of evidence on them though, we would be able to send them away for the rest of their lives and they would be another pair of cunts off the streets.

So far, there hadn't been any evidence linking them to Morpheus or Ettore, which was an interesting turn of events. Merza was at the hospital with Arcadia and the first group of kids that we had saved. From what Kade had told us their condition was far worse than we could even imagine. The kids had been used as science experiments. Merza said that their stories were so hard to hear, and she wasn't sure even how to go about helping them. I worried that this was going to be a group of kids that would be stuck forever living in a psychiatric unit because they were too messed up.

Anghus and the rest of the Devil's Advocates have been integral in helping omegas that had escaped or been rescued from breeding facilities. But in my time at the AJE authority, we had never come up against a case like this one. No one knew how these kids were going to be in the end. It was a terrifying thought.

Pulling up to the driveway on Tomlinson Road, I saw that the Devil's Advocates were already there. We climbed out of the van and joined Anghus who was standing with Lynx, and a few of the other inner Devils.

"Israel has gone in with Scout to let us know what to expect," Anghus said as Kade joined us.

"Excellent, the more we know the smoother this raid will go," Kade replied.

"How are the kids?" Lynx asked.

Kade shook his head and sighed. "I don't know if they are ever going to be alright. They were tortured. None of them have eyes. The ones that were shifters were given silver so they couldn't shift. They have missing limbs and others have crude wings implanted into their backs. The doctors are slowly trying to work out what each child has or doesn't have."

"Fucking hell," Anghus said with a shake of his head.

"Yep. Merza said one little girl is a wolf shifter, she thinks the girl is about nine or ten. She has full-sized adult gargoyle wings attached to her back and is in a permanent half-shifted state."

My eyes widened and my mouth dropped open. "How the hell is that possible?"

Kade shrugged his shoulders. "I don't know. Arcadia is working with councils and doctors to try and work out what is going on. It's almost like the little girl is a hybrid. She can't talk or even barely open her mouth. It's horrifying."

"Do you know anything more about those people?" Anghus asked.

Kade shook his head. "Not yet. The human team is interviewing them, but now they aren't giving anything away. Arcadia has been busy with the kids but when she gets a chance, she is going to attempt to read them. Hopefully, that will give us a better understanding of what is going on. The eldest girl we believe is twenty-two. We don't know where she came from. She said she doesn't remember anything before being with Archibald and Elizabeth. She had been kept in a cage all her life and had only recently been moved to the new cage."

"How did they get them here without ever being caught?" I asked.

"The girl, who doesn't have a name, or at least doesn't know what it is, said that they were loaded onto a large vehicle. I'm assuming a truck. They traveled for a long time in a container."

"Fucking hell, this is disgusting," Anghus growled with a shake of his head. "I want to fucking gut them."

"You and me both man," Kade replied. It was a sentiment we all shared. It was about an hour later that Scout flew overhead with Israel in their claws. They flew down and landed beside the vans, before shifting into human form.

"What were you able to find out?" Kade asked as Israel took a pair of jeans from Jai and Scout slipped on a pair of sweatpants.

"There are people in the building. Same set up as the other property," Israel answered.

"Lily?" I asked.

Israel nodded his head. "Yeah, she is in there. She's in a cage with two others. But I'm warning you, Nash, prepare yourself. The ones she's in a cage with are Alphas."

My eyes widened and a groan fell from my lips.

"Shit," Anghus swore. "Has she been raped?"

Israel nodded his head. "And wears mating marks."

"Fuck," I roared as I turned and thrust my hands up through my hair in anger. I was going to fucking kill them. I was going to tear them to pieces, thread by fucking thread. Lily was fucking twelve years old. Too young to understand mates. Too young to be bred.

"Nash, we can fix this," Oakland said quietly. "It won't take back the pain and anguish she has felt, but we can break the mating bond with very little pain."

I nodded my head and glanced up at the warlock. "Thank you."

Oakland nodded his head and reached out a hand giving my shoulder a squeeze. I didn't know how I was going to break the news to Papa. This was just about the worst thing that could have happened to her. In fact, I can't help but feel it would have been better if she had been killed.

"How many other alphas are in there?" Kade was asking Israel.

"Two to every cage, with one omega. In all I counted seven omegas, so fourteen alphas."

"Alright, we will wait for the rest of the Rebels to arrive and the vampire team. We are going to need to disable the alphas. I don't know what to expect with this, the fact that the alphas have been locked with the omegas is strange. We need to be prepared for anything," Kade said as he pulled his phone from his pocket and placed it against his ear. "Travis, we need all of you guys on Tomlinson road. I'll brief you when you get here."

Chapter Twenty-Nine

Maddox

I'd gone home and laid in bed as Nash instructed, but no matter how much I tried, sleep wasn't about to come. I was worried sick. Not just for Lily but also for Nash. I was worried for everyone on their team. I was worried for the young omegas that were taken from the first property. Nash hadn't gone into details about their condition, but he'd used the word torture. That made me envision all sorts of horrible things.

I felt useless laying in bed staring at the ceiling, but I knew I was too exhausted to work. Carl and Brandt had said they'd go and check on the other crews to give me a chance to rest, but I almost wish I hadn't agreed to it. My mind was spinning at a million miles an hour and I needed to do something to keep my mind off what was going on in the outside world.

I picked up my phone and opened the chat log I had with Alexander. *How is everything going?* I sent. I wasn't sure whether he was going to be involved with the raid on the second property or not.

They found Lily apparently. That other property had omegas and alphas in it. I can't say more than that though. Alexander's text came back almost immediately.

I frowned at the screen. In the shifter world, alphas were the unspoken leaders. They were the ones that were traditionally at the head. For there to be alphas locked away with the omegas didn't make a lot of sense.

I'm glad they found her. I replied to Alexander. I wanted to send a text through to Nash but wasn't sure that it would be the best thing to do. I hoped that Lily was alright and hadn't been tortured like the others. I hoped that this might mend the fences between Nash and his family.

What a way to meet your eldest brother. To be abducted and held prisoner for a few days. I sighed. The poor kid. An image of my own father floated through my mind. I wondered if he would have done the same for me. *Would he have bothered to come looking if I'd been abducted?* Part of me liked to hope he would have, but then the other part thought, that there was a possibility he'd blame me for getting taken.

I sometimes thought about whether I should attempt to contact my father. To show him what success I'd become without him. To perhaps throw it in his face that I was nothing like him. *But what good would it do?* For the mere minutes of satisfaction, it might provide me, in the end, it wouldn't really fix anything.

I wondered if he and Mama went on to have more children. Or if Mama reconnected with her family once I was gone. The one who didn't ask to be raped but got the blame for it anyway. Sometimes I thought about trying to find a way to contact Mama without Papa knowing, but then I remembered that she never fought for me. She stood there and watched as Papa threw me out of the house. Fuck, she even knew that I was being raped and sat in the other room while it happened.

I scoffed and shook my head, sighing deeply. I walked over to the couch and flopped into the comfortable cushion, flicking on the television. The news broadcast that I'd been watching the day before was still on, but this time the banner read, "Lily Andrews found." I smiled at the screen as I read the scrolling script that floated at the bottom of the television.

A knock on the door roused me out of my thoughts and when I swung the door open, I saw that Carter was on the other side. My best friend stopped and cocked his head to the side and looked at me with a frown.

"You haven't slept," Carter growled.

I almost wanted to roll my eyes and stomp my foot like a petulant child at being called out, instead I nodded my head and moved aside so that Carter could come in through the front door.

"The little girl that was abducted, was Nash's little sister. I was worried about her, and about Nash," I explained.

Carter sat down on the couch that I'd just moved from, and I flopped down beside him, kicking my legs out in front of me and resting my feet on the coffee table.

"I didn't think he spoke to his family," Carter replied.

I shook my head. "No, he didn't. But his Papa rang Nash when it was discovered Lily was missing. It put them back in contact. I don't know if they will keep in contact now that Lily has been found."

"I hope they do. I hate families being pulled apart. Generally, it is always over a minor issue that didn't need to occur in the first place."

I chuckled and nodded my head. "Yeah, like going to trade school to become a carpenter."

Carter nodded. "Exactly like that. You're a strong man Maddox to have been able to do without your family. I'm not sure I'd be the same."

"I had Tom and Margaret."

"That's true, but it isn't the same as having those that biologically raised you."

I hummed and glanced over at Carter with a shrug. "Maybe. But at least Tom never beat the shit out of me. If I did something that disappointed them, they would sit down and converse with me and listen to my side of the story. Papa never did any of those things. He led with his fist."

"Yeah, and I still fucking hate that cunt for it."

I smiled and nodded. "Me too."

Chapter Thirty

Nash

My stomach was churning as Scout led Lily out of the building. The shifter unit had tried to enter but the alphas became feral. They had snarled and spat at us as we went towards the cages. We'd had to retreat and allow Scout and the vampire team to enter.

"Lily," I said quietly as the little girl was led towards the medics. Her clothes were literally hanging onto her body with threads. Her body was covered in bite marks. Her eyes were red and puffy from her tears. Blood stained her legs, and I knew that she had been torn up. The thought made my stomach revolt. The two alphas that walked beside her glared at me and curled their lips in threat.

"I don't want your omega," I said pushing my alpha voice over. "I'm her biological brother."

The two alphas relaxed slightly and stood back to allow Lily to step forward. She looked at me and a small sob fell from her lips. "Nash?" she whispered.

"Yes, little one. I'm Nash."

Lily cried again and stepped into me circling her arms around my middle in a tight hug. My eyes burned with tears as I kissed the top of her head. They had hurt her so badly. My heart was tearing apart in my chest. I didn't know what we were going to do. I didn't know how to fix it.

"How badly are you hurt?" I asked pulling her away from my chest to look down into her face.

Her green eyes looked dead as she looked up at me. "I'm hurt. Bad."

I nodded my head and looked over at the alphas who were watching me with narrowed eyes. "Who are you, men?" I asked.

They glanced between each other and then looked back at me. "We don't have a name," one of them answered.

I frowned. "Have you always been with Archibald and Elizabeth?"

They both nodded their heads in unison. "Did you come with them from Sydney?"

They shrugged, the one who answered me previously was the one to speak again. "I don't know where we came from. We were brought here and told to make her our mate."

I glanced down at Lily and sighed. These alphas were victims just as Lily was. "Are all the alphas the same as you?" I asked as I watched Scout gently leading another omega with two alphas over to Kaylee.

They nodded their heads again. "I didn't want to mate with her," the other alpha said. "I didn't want to hurt her. But if we didn't, we would have been killed."

I sighed. "Do you know how old you are?"

They both shook their heads. I could feel their fear and anguish in their body language. The whole scenario was horrible. And it was only Archibald and Elizabeth's fault.

"What kind of supernatural are you?" I asked.

"I'm a centaur and my brother is a griffin," the first alpha answered.

"And you were born and raised in the place with Archibald and Elizabeth?"

"Yes, we don't remember a time before then."

I hummed and glanced back down at Lily before looking back up at them. "Do you understand that Lily is only twelve years old? She is too young to be mated. She isn't old enough to breed."

The two alphas sighed and nodded their heads. "Did we do wrong?" one of them asked.

"Yes, but no. You did but, you were made to do it, I don't know what the answer is, to be honest. But please understand that we need to break the mating."

"I understand," the alpha that did most of the talking said. "What will happen to us?"

"I don't know," I replied as Kade approached.

"Is she safe?" he asked.

"Yes. They understand that we need to break the mating," I explained.

Kade nodded and gave the alphas a gentle smile. "Let's get you both checked by the medic then we will work with Merza and Oakland to break the mating."

The alphas nodded their heads and allowed Kade to lead them over to where Kaylee was waiting. I looked down at Lily who hadn't let go of me since she was brought towards me.

"Don't leave me, Nash," she pleaded.

I smiled down at her and stroked my hand over her head. "I'm not going anywhere, little one. I'll ring Papa and Stacey soon to let them know that we've found you."

"Mama will be mad," she said with a small sob.

I shook my head. "Why would she be angry?"

"Because I'm mated, I'm probably pregnant. Mama said that if I ever got pregnant, she would be furious with me. She didn't want me to have children."

"Oh Lily," I replied with a shake of my head. Stacey was a bitch. "No matter what Stacey says, I'm not leaving your side. I promise."

"Thank you, Nash."

I smiled and stroked my hand down over her head again. My heart ached even more. This poor kid had been through a horrible ordeal and still worried that her Mama would reject her for something that wasn't even in her control.

Chapter Thirty-One

After a lot of convincing from both Kaylee and me, Lily let me go long enough that Kaylee could look her over and I could ring Papa.

"Nash," Papa answered immediately.

"Papa, we've found Lily," I replied.

Papa let out a sob. "Is she. Is she alive?"

"Yes. But she isn't unharmed," I said as I tried to find a way to break it to my father that his youngest daughter had been raped and brutalized.

"She is alive, that is all that matters, we can help her with the rest."

"Yes. She is with the medic now, but she has been mated. The alphas are victims too but have agreed to break the mating. We will be working with Merza Sinclair and Oakland Reece from the Devil's Advocates. They will break the mating."

"Oh," Papa said, and I could hear shuffling in the background. "Is she pregnant?"

"I don't know. Kaylee will be doing checks to see if she is."

"Alright."

"Papa, Lily is scared that Stacey will reject her if she is pregnant. That she is going to be angry at Lily for being raped. Is this true?"

"Son, Stacey has some strong opinions about things. She doesn't see things as openly as the young ones do. Things like being pregnant young or being raped aren't as shameful as it was when she was young."

"Being raped hasn't been shameful ever Papa. It is not Lily's fault. She didn't do anything wrong here," I argued.

"I know son. I know. But Stacey doesn't see it that way."

"So, you are saying that Stacey is going to reject her own daughter because of something that she couldn't control?"

Papa sighed and cleared his throat. "I don't know son. It is possible, but I can't say."

"Do not let that woman anywhere near Lily, if she is going to reject her. That little girl has been through too much to have her mother blaming her for this shit," I growled.

"Where will she go?" Papa sighed, sounding defeated.

"She can come home with me and my mate. We will get her the help she needs, but I won't tolerate her being blamed for something that was out of her control."

"Alright, Nash. I will speak to Stacey and then I will ring you. I'm sorry son. I'm sorry."

"Don't be sorry Papa, just do better," I growled before ending the call.

I was furious. That bitch. *How could anyone possibly blame a child for something that was completely out of her fucking control?*

"Nash?" Kaylee called. I glanced over to the tent that was set up and saw that Kaylee was standing outside the door. Merza and Oakland were sitting with Lily. Merza had Lily's hand in her as Oakland held his hand gently over her head and his lips moved as he spoke a spell over her.

"Is she alright?" I asked.

Kaylee sighed and shook her head. "She was brutalized. Badly. She isn't pregnant, but I don't think she will ever get pregnant. They have destroyed her insides beyond what her healing power could keep up with. She wasn't anywhere near going into heats yet."

I growled and ran my hands up over my face. "I want to fucking kill them, but it's not their fault either. I fucking hate this shit."

"Me too," Kaylee said. "They have been just as badly tortured."

I frowned. "How so?"

"From talking to them, they were first taught how to breed by being forced to mate with each other. And have alphas taking them. They were only taught brutal."

I growled again and shook my head. "Those cunts need to rot in fucking hell."

"They will. They are going to be tried in the supernatural courts rather than the human courts," Kade said as he stepped in beside me. "How is she?"

Kaylee shook her head. "Not good. Physically she will eventually heal. I don't think she will ever have children or even go into heat. But mentally, Nash, she is going to need a lot of therapy."

"I will make sure she gets it," I said.

"Have you spoken to your father?" Kade asked.

I nodded my head. "His mate is likely to reject Lily," I said with a sneer.

Kaylee gasped and her eyes widened. "Are you fucking kidding?"

I shook my head. "Nope. Apparently being raped in Stacey's mind is the victims fucking fault. Papa said he was going to ring me back once he'd talked to Stacey."

As if on cue, my phone rang and when I looked at the screen, I saw Papa's ID come up. "Papa," I answered.

"I'm sorry Nash. Take Lily home. Love her. Be the best parent you can be. Be a better parent than I ever was," Papa said.

I shook my head with disgust. "Where are your balls Papa, you have now let that woman run off two of your children," I snapped. "Why won't you stand up to her?"

"I love her Nash. I was broken when your Mama died. Stacey is all I have left."

"Fuck that. Your children are supposed to mean more than the pussy that you're fucking," I growled.

"I'm sorry Nash. I really am. Please don't bring Lily around, and please don't come back home."

I slammed my thumb onto the end call button and growled. "Fuck," I spat.

Kade reached out an arm and pulled me into his chest. "Do not let that little girl feel your anger. Stay calm for her. Just for now. Go and ring Maddox, let him know what is about to happen, and take the time to calm down. That little girl needs you and she needs that Dad, I know you are."

I nodded my head as my eyes stung with tears. Kade was right. Lily didn't deserve to witness my anger. She needed my love; she needed my protection. She needed everything that my Papa and Stacey failed to give her.

Kade let me go and I walked away with a quick glimpse over at Lily who was still holding tightly to Merza's hand while Oakland continued to work on breaking the mating. My tears fell over my cheeks and my heart tore that little bit more. This was fucked. The whole scenario was fucked.

Chapter Thirty-Two

Maddox

I was curled up on the couch after Carter forced me to lie down in front of cartoons with my pacifier so that I would stop stressing about Nash when my phone rang. Carter looked at the screen.

"It's Nash," he said handing it over to me.

I sat up and spat my pacifier out and pressed the answer button. "Nash, is everything alright?"

"Yes and no baby. We found Lily, she is alive, but she had been mated. Oakland and Merza are breaking the mating now. I rang Papa and that cunt of a stepmother is rejecting Lily because she was raped."

"What the fuck?" I squawked. "How the fuck do you reject your child for something that isn't in her control?" I realized the irony in what I was saying as soon as I said it. My Papa had done exactly the same thing to me. But it was something I knew I would never do to my own child and was horrified to think that there was another parent as callous as my Papa out there.

"That's how I feel too."

"What are you going to do?" I asked.

"Well, I wanted to ring to ask," Nash started.

"Bring her home, Nash. She needs love and support. Bring her home."

"We haven't really talked about where home is yet baby," he said with a chuckle.

"Oh, I suppose we haven't. Do you want to move in here? I mean I can move over with you if that is what you would rather, it's just that with my workshop and that it will take some time to sort things out."

"No baby, I will move in there. I live in a one-bedroom apartment. But I want to make sure you are serious. You might be pregnant, and then to have a twelve-year-old that has been to hell and back, that is a lot to expect of you."

"Nash, she needs a home. She needs love. She needs family. You are the only biological family she is going to be left with. You and I both know how it feels to have our family turn their backs on us and how much that hurts. If we can ease that pain for her somewhat then I want to do that."

"Thank you, baby. You are a beautiful man," he said with a sigh.

"You are too, my love."

"Thank you. I must go and get back to Lily, but I will bring her home once she has finished with all the tests and breaking the mating."

"Alright, I'll see you when you get home," I said as I ended the call and looked over at Carter.

"I'm guessing that Nash found his sister and it wasn't good," Carter said.

I nodded my head. "She was forced mated and raped. But Nash's father and stepmother have rejected her. From what I can tell they blame Lily for being raped."

Carter growled in his throat. "That's fucked."

"Yeah, it is. Nash is going to bring her here."

"Are you thinking this through? I know that you love strongly, but this girl is going to have a lot of issues."

"I know, but what other option is there? If Nash doesn't take her, she will be likely thrown into the foster system. I mean at best, we could probably get her over to the Devil's Advocates, but that's even not as good as being with her brother."

"A brother she has never met until today," Carter reminded me.

I sighed and nodded my head. "I feel that this is the right thing to do. I don't know if it is the creator pushing me or if it is my head, but I just feel that it's the right thing to do. We will get her the help she needs."

Carter smiled and reached out a hand and grasped my shoulder. "You're a good man Maddox. You do know you're probably going to need to learn to cook now though."

I barked out a laugh. "Maybe my Daddy can teach me." My eyes widened and I gasped as I looked down at my pacifier that sat in my lap.

"Bring it up with her slowly. She will understand. Explain to Lily that this is your way to cope with your own shitty childhood."

I nodded my head. "Not right away. She needs to start her healing process first."

"There is time. Plenty of time yet."

I smiled and nodded at my best friend. We had a whole lifetime.

Chapter Thirty-Three

Nash

I felt somewhat better by the time I got off the phone to Maddox. I didn't know what it was about my mate but just hearing his voice soothed the angry alpha inside me that wanted to rip my father and stepmother's heads off. Merza was still sitting beside Lily holding her hand, while Kaylee sat on the other side rubbing her back.

The three looked up at me. Merza smiled warmly as I approached. "Lily was just telling me she loves writing stories."

I smiled. "That's amazing. I'd love to read some of your stories sometime."

"They are all at home," she said quietly. I winced and tried to school my face, but I was too slow. Lily noticed and nodded her head. "She doesn't want me does she."

"I'm sorry Lily," I said with a sigh. "I tried to speak sense to Papa."

Lily hiccupped a small sob and I noticed the tears that welled up in her big green eyes. It made me want to kill my father all over again.

"Where will I go?"

"Well, you have a choice and I'm going to let you choose," I started. "I have a mate, named Maddox, he has a house in Lalbert and said that if you'd like you could live with us. I've only just met him myself, so I'd be moving in there too."

Lily smiled and nodded her head. "I know Maddox, he came to our school sometimes to do lessons for woodwork class."

I smiled, grateful that Lily knew my mate, and by the look on her face, he'd made a good impression on her. "That is one of the choices. Another choice is that you could live with other omegas who have been through similar experiences as you. Some were raised in breeding facilities. They live in a big compound with the Devil's Advocates," I said as I glanced around for Anghus. Spotting him I pointed over at the huge gargoyle that was helping Kade keep control of some alphas. "See the big guy next to Kade? He is the president of the Devil's Advocates."

Lily nodded her head but the frown on her face said that she didn't like the idea of living with the Devils. "The other option is that we can find you a foster family to live with."

Lily wrinkled her nose and shook her head. "The Devil's Advocates, do they have other kids there my age?"

I felt my gut tighten in disappointment but made sure not to show it on my face. This was Lily's choice.

"They do. They have a school there also that they have specifically for supernatural kids."

Lily bit into her lip and glanced again at Anghus. "And Maddox? He really wouldn't mind if I came to live with you?"

I shook my head. "Not at all. In fact, he practically demanded it, but I wanted to give you the options. I think you've had enough people demanding things from you for now."

Lily nodded. "Only bad things. Maddox isn't demanding bad things, is he?"

I shook my head. "Absolutely not. No matter where you choose to live, I can guarantee that you will always be protected. If you choose our home or the Devil's Advocates. I trust Anghus and the other Devils completely and I know that you would be safe there. And I trust Maddox implicitly and know that you would be safe in our home."

Lily bit into her bottom lip again and glanced over at Anghus once more before she nodded her head. "I want to live with you. But Nash? Can I visit the kids at the Devil's Advocates sometimes? And the omegas that have been through what I have?"

I smiled and nodded. "Absolutely. I know that the kids would love to have you in their friendship group. And if you wanted to go to the school there, I'm happy to take you out there and pick you up every day."

"Can I think about that?"

"Of course, you can. You take as long as you like."

"Will Papa let me get my things do you think? I don't care about my clothes, but I'd like my stories."

"I'll ask. If not, he might be willing to let some of the AJE authority there."

"I'll go," Merza said with a smile. "I'll grab you everything that is in your bedroom hey?"

Lily smiled and her eyes lit up for the first time as she bounced her head up and down. "Thank you. I'd like that."

Merza gave Lily's hand a squeeze and stood from the stretcher she'd been sitting on. "I'll grab Arcadia and head out there now. Between the two of us, I'm sure we can make that awful woman give it up."

"Thank you, Merza. That means a lot to me," I replied with a smile. I knew how convincing Merza and Arcadia could be. They were a force to be reckoned with.

"Anytime sweetheart."

"Can I go back to your house now Nash?" Lily asked. I glanced over at Kaylee who nodded her head.

"I'm finished with all my tests, I'll pass the results onto Dr. Osbourne, and he will probably make an appointment for Lily, just in case there are any follow-up tests that need to be done."

"Thanks, Kaylee. I'll bring her in anytime."

Kaylee turned to Lily and stroked her hand gently over her hair. "I am glad that you're safe now Lily. Nash and Maddox are wonderful people and I'm so happy that you are going to have the opportunity to live and grow there."

Lily smiled. "Thank you, Kaylee. I'm glad that I'm going to be living with them too."

Chapter Thirty-Four

Maddox

It had been two weeks since Lily came to us. I was filled with disgust for her parents. They hadn't once contacted her and from what Merza said she had a battle just to be able to get the girl's clothes. I mean the poor kid came home from being raped and brutalized wearing a pair of scrubs because her clothes had been destroyed. The mother didn't want to give her any of her belongings. It disgusted me.

Finally, after Merza threatened to haul her ass into AJE on charges, Stacey relented and let Merza and Arcadia collect her clothes and notebooks. Stacey hadn't let them take anything else. So, Nash bought her a new laptop and phone. She stayed home with me, I'd organized with Carl and Brandt to take over management for a few weeks while I settled Lily into the house.

Nash had to work, there was a lot to do regarding the kids they discovered. From what they had been able to find out, the kids were used as science experiments. Arcadia was able to discover that Archie was a retired scientist who had been studying hybrids and how to manipulate the genetics in the supernatural to create the ultimate supernatural.

There had been countless children killed under his and Elizabeth's hands. Those few that survived were the ones that were found in the shed. From what they were able to discover the AJE authority in Sydney had been investigating them. Archibald and Elizabeth had become aware of the investigation and fled. The children that they brought with them were all the ones they currently had in their care. They'd piled them up in the back of a truck container and basically had them delivered to Lalbert.

Lily was taken on a whim. Archibald has never said what it was about Lily that attracted him, but the first time he'd seen her was in the supermarket. After that he started stalking her, waiting for the right time to take her. From there he took her to the property that my team was supposed to start building on and thrust her in a cage with two alphas who were told to rape her. Well, they were told to mate with her.

We'd taken Lily for an appointment with Dr. Osbourne who had confirmed that she wasn't pregnant and unfortunately would have a great deal of trouble ever getting pregnant again. Lily said that she would never mate with anyone so it didn't bother her, but I wondered if that was something that would change in the future.

Every night she woke with nightmares. I'd sit up with her and hold her while she sobbed in my arms. She told me a lot of what happened to her during her time in the cage. It was horrific. From what I understood from Lily and Nash, the alphas were practically feral. They didn't understand anything about societal rules. Lily told me that they hadn't wanted to mate with her, but they were made to by Archie. I felt my heartbreak for the alphas too. I hated Archibald and Elizabeth for what they did. They made this little girl witness things she should never see. She has lived through things that would break most people. I couldn't believe how strong she was.

Lily had started seeing a therapist who she liked a lot. Alexandria was wonderful, she'd been great for Landon, Israel's mate who had been raped. Lily had felt comfortable opening to Alexandria and seemed to be healing every day. She still had a long way to go, but I could see some of the light starting to come back in her eyes. I believed her when she said that she would never take on another mate. I prayed to Mother fate that she would hold off for Lily. I trusted that the creator wouldn't push a mating on someone that wasn't ready, but I figured the extra request would help.

I still hadn't admitted to Lily about my little side. I knew that I was going to have to have that conversation with her. I knew that I wasn't going to be able to hide it forever. I needed my little side. It was a comfort to me. We were sitting watching cartoons on the couch and I was lost in them when I decided it was time to have the conversation.

"Hey Lily," I said. Lily turned to me with a smile. "Can I talk to you about something?"

"Of course," she said as she flipped the switch on the remote to turn the television off.

"Well, when I was very little, I went through something very similar to you. Instead of it being strangers though, it was my uncle. My father blamed me for what happened. As a result of what my uncle did, my Mama's family turned their back on her and my Papa. He blamed me for losing the money that Mama's family had. He mistreated me as a result, when I was seventeen, I was kicked out of my house. I was lucky and was taken in by a human couple who cared for and loved me. I was able to get therapy. The way that I ended up dealing with things that happened to me, was that I found myself reverting."

Lily frowned and cocked her head to the side. "Reverting?"

I nodded my head. "When my brain becomes too stressed or I need a break from reality, my brain sends me back to an age that I felt most safe, which is around about eighteen months. I like to dress in footy pajamas, watch cartoons and suck on a pacifier. Sometimes I might wear a diaper."

"Oh," Lily said. The frown pulled at her brow as she thought over what I had told her. I bit on my bottom lip. My stomach rolled as I wondered how she was going to react. "Does it help you?"

I nodded my head. "Yeah."

"And Nash knows about it?"

I nodded again. "He does. When we became mated, he took on the role of my Daddy so to speak, he takes care of me."

Lily bit on her bottom lip. "But he isn't your mate when you are little?"

I shook my head. "No. I don't do anything that involves sex while I'm little."

Lily nodded. "I think I get it. I can understand why you would want that. I think I like the idea of staying eleven before everything happened. Before it was hard."

"That's right, that's how it feels for me."

"Do you need to be little now?" Lily asked.

I shook my head. "No. But I just wanted you to know so that if there comes a time that I do need to, or if you stumble across a pacifier that I forget to put away, it doesn't freak you out."

Lily smiled. "Thank you for talking to me about it, like I'm a grown-up."

I lifted my arm and allowed her to snuggle into my side. I kissed the top of her head. Unfortunately, this event means that she has had to grow up so much faster than she should have.

Lily lifted her face and looked up at me. "Do you think you're pregnant?"

"Oh, you know what, with everything that has gone on, I haven't even thought to check," I said with a laugh. "Would you be upset if I was?"

Lily smiled and shook her head. "Not at all. I would help look after the baby. You would make a great Dad. You and Nash."

"Thank you little one," I said kissing the top of her head again. "Do you feel up to going to the store with me?"

Lily quickly shook her head. "I'm scared."

"That's okay. You don't have to go. How about instead, we go to the Devil's compound, they are bound to have loads of pregnancy tests there."

Lily smiled and nodded. "Thank you."

I patted my knees as I stood from the couch. "Alright, let's get going. I'll text Nash and let him know where we are."

Lily bounced off the couch and dashed into the room which we had made hers for her shoes. The room was still plain and didn't contain more than a bed and wardrobe. I had talked to her about setting it up into a paradise for her, but we hadn't got any further.

Chapter Thirty-Five

I quickly text Nash and he replied with a smiley face emoji followed by kisses and then an exciting-looking selfie that made me laugh. On the way to the Devil's Advocates compound, I noticed that Lily continued to twist and fidget with her fingers.

"Are you alright?" I asked. "We don't have to go to the compound if you're not comfortable."

Lily looked up at me and shook her head. "I'm alright. Just nervous. This is the first time I've been out since Nash brought me home."

I reached out my hand and gently took hers in mine. "I will protect you. You are safe at the Devil's compound." Lily nodded her head but didn't say anything. "How about we think about your room while we are driving?" I suggested.

"Alright," she replied with a small smile. I hadn't seen more than that small smile come from her since she came to us, but every day it seemed to get a little easier for her to let it free.

"What's your favorite color?" I asked.

Lily hummed and tapped her finger on her chin. "I really like purple."

"I love purple too. I really like purple and black mixed together."

Lily's eyes widened and she bounced her head up and down. "Yes, like that color of dawn, right before the sun starts cresting."

I grinned. "I love it. Do you like art?"

"I'm not very good at it. I'm better at writing."

"That's alright. I have a friend March. He is an artist and so very good at it. His mate's brother Burgess is a tattoo artist. They are both omegas. If you feel comfortable, we could speak to them about designing a scene for you. Burgess and March did a beautiful nursery for Burgess's children that he not long ago had."

Lily smiled and nodded her head. "I would like that."

"Great," I replied with a grin. "I'll give March a text. I warn you that he is excitable. You know how I'm a little? Well, March is a middle, so he reverts to his teenage years. He tends to be a bit like a teen boy."

Lily let out a little giggle. "I like that. You said he has a mate?"

"Yes. Asher Rigby. He is a nice guy, a bear shifter."

Lily covered her lips and giggled again. "I know of Asher Rigby."

My eyes widened. "How on earth do you know about Asher?"

Lily rolled her eyes. It was the most animated I'd ever seen her, and I was loving it. "Everyone that is everyone knows Asher and his kinky club. Wait do you and Nash go there?"

I chuckled and shook my head. "No. Well, I don't. Nash is a member there."

Lily scrunched her nose. "Yuck, I wish I hadn't asked."

I barked out a laugh. "He doesn't go anymore."

Lily smiled. "He doesn't need to. He has the perfect mate at home."

I grinned. "And the perfect little sister and hopefully baby."

Lily's smile grew to the biggest I'd ever seen. I wanted to capture the moment. She was gorgeous at that moment. All her worries appeared to have been lost. Her eyes sparkled with that fae mischief.

"Do you think you will have a boy or a girl?"

I hummed. "I don't know. I don't mind what we have. What would you like?"

Lily hummed. "Both. Oh, wait no. I want you to have quadruplets."

I nearly swerved the car off the road as I swung my head to look at Lily who giggled. "Quadruplets?"

Lily bounced her head up and down. "Yep, two boys and two girls."

"I'm not sure my belly would be big enough to fill with four babies."

"Your skin will stretch."

I laughed and shook my head as I took the turn to pull into the Devil's Advocates compound. I slowed as I reached the guardhouse and smiled when I saw that it was Miles on duty.

"Hey Maddox, I didn't know you were coming," he said with a grin.

"It was a bit of a last-minute decision. I'm hoping that Larissa might have a spare pregnancy test at the medical unit."

Miles's eyes widened and he wolf-whistled. "You and Nash been busy?"

I barked out a laugh. "Gross," Lily groaned from the passenger seat.

Miles ducked down to look in the car. His cheeks blushed and he chuckled. "Sorry, I didn't know that Maddox wasn't alone."

"This is Lily, she is Nash's," I started.

"Daughter," Lily finished before looking at me with a smile. "I'm Nash and Maddox's daughter."

Miles seemed to already know what Lily's story was, it was all over the news, but they had also taken in the omegas that were found.

"It's awesome to meet you, Lily. My name is Miles. I'm one of the Devil's Advocates. Will you be coming to our school?"

Lily shrugged and started to fidget her hands again. "I don't know."

"No hurry on any decisions," Miles said with a smile. "I'll let the two of you go so that you can go search down a pregnancy test. If all else fails, Iver is at the main house. He will tell you."

"I must thank Iver. He was the one that set me and Nash on the right path."

Miles barked out a laugh. "Yeah, that kid is something amazing."

I nodded my head and pulled away from the guardhouse and along the driveway towards where the medical unit was.

"Who is Iver?" Lily asked.

"He is Anghus, Bacchus and Joachim's son. He was born a cthulu. He is seven. But so powerful. He can converse directly to the creator."

"Wow," Lily gasped. "This place is really beautiful."

"It sure is. They have worked hard to make it a place of peace and security."

"I like that. And the school it is here?"

"Sure is," I said as I pointed at the large school building. "See that log building there?"

Lily nodded her head and leaned forward to watch as the kids came running out of the building, they were laughing and playing.

"Oh, they are all different ages," Lily noted.

"Yes. There are a few kids that are the same age as you." Lily nodded but didn't say anymore. I pulled into the front of the medical unit and killed the engine. "Want to come inside with me and meet Larissa?"

"Okay," Lily said sucking in a deep breath before reaching out to the handle and swinging the door open.

As the doors shut on the car, Iver looked up and a smile grew on his lips. He came running towards us but stopped short, not encroaching into Lily's space.

"Hi Maddox, Hi Lily," he said.

Lily's eyes widened. "How did you know my name?"

Iver giggled. "The creator told me you were coming. I was waiting for you. Would you like to come and meet the other kids?"

Lily twisted her hands in front of her and glanced over at me. "It's up to you. If you would like to, you are welcome to, or if you would prefer to come with me you can do that too."

"Wait," Iver said before he turned. "Rhyland? Five? Six?"

Three kids looked up and came running over to Iver. Rhyland, I knew but the kids named Five and Six I didn't know. Iver turned back to Lily with a smile. "This is Rhyland, he is a firefly shifter, this is Five, he is a phoenix shifter and Six is a siren. Rhyland is fourteen, Five is thirteen, and Six is twelve. This is Lily, she is fae."

"Hi Lily," Six answered.

"Hi, Six."

"We are going to do some painting soon; would you like to come and paint with us?" Rhyland asked.

Lily glanced at me, and I shrugged my shoulders. "Will you be far away?" she asked.

I shook my head. "No. I'm just going into the building to do a pregnancy test and then I'll come and find you."

"You don't have to do a pregnancy test, Maddox," Iver said with a laugh.

I raised my brow at the boy. "Is he pregnant?" Five asked.

Iver nodded his head. "But don't tell Papa that I told you. He keeps saying I must learn not to blurt everything."

"Does he have quadruplets?" Lily asked with a giggle making me roll my eyes.

Iver shook his head. "Nope, but there is more than one."

"How many more than one?" I questioned.

Iver laughed and Lily clapped her hands. "Quintuplets? Sextuplets?"

I coughed and shook my head. "No, don't make it more."

Lily threw her head back and laughed again.

"There are two," Iver said with a grin.

I sighed out a breath and placed my hand on my chest. "Thank the gods."

"Wanna know what they are?" Iver asked.

"Sure, hit me up," I said with a laugh.

"Two girls. They are going to be identical in all but one way."

Lily grinned and spun to me. "That's so exciting. Maybe we can ask March to decorate their nursery too. In unicorn colors."

"Woah," Iver said. "Can you talk to the baby's spirits too?"

Lily frowned and shook her head. "No."

"How did you know they were going to be unicorns though?"

"I didn't."

Iver smiled. "It was the babies spirits telling you. You just didn't realize it. If you decide to come to our school, you will learn how to do that."

Lily's eyes widened and she gasped. "Really? I can do that?"

Iver nodded his head. "Yep. Everyone has magic."

"Wow," Lily whispered.

"Alright kids, we are going to start art class now," Burgess called out as he came out of the main house and down the front steps with a baby on each hip. "Oh, hey Maddox, it's good to see you, man."

I walked towards him with a smile. "The babies have grown so much."

Burgess nodded his head. "They sure have." Thatcher and Saffron chewed on their chubby fists as they curled into Burgess. "I hear that you have a little girl that you and Nash have unofficially adopted."

I nodded my head and turned. Lily was still talking to Iver, Rhyland, Five, and Six. "Yes, Lily. Do you mind if she joined in on the art class?"

"Of course, man, the more the merrier. What brings you here anyway?"

"Well, a pregnancy test, but the walking pregnancy test just told me that I am indeed pregnant with identical twin girls," I said with a laugh.

Burgess threw his head back with a laugh. "I love that kid."

"Me too. They are awesome."

Lily walked over to me and smiled up at Burgess before leaning into my side. "Would you like to stay for the art class?" I asked.

Lily nodded her head. "Yes please."

"Excellent. My name is Burgess. It's wonderful to meet you, Lily. This is Thatcher and Saffron," Burgess introduced.

Saffron took that moment to throw herself out of Burgess's arms. Lily caught the little girl with a gasp.

"Oh girl," Burgess sighed. "You are the queen of giving people heart attacks." Lily laughed and bounced Saffron on her hip as the baby nuzzled into Lily's neck. "She is always throwing herself out of my arms to get to people she wants to snuggle with."

"Lucky Lily is a good catch," I laughed.

Lily looked up at me and smiled. "Alright, well let's get to doing some art so that Maddox can go and do the pregnancy test just to make sure that Iver is right."

Lily nodded her head. "Will we be just there?" she asked Burgess.

"Yes, we are just going to be in that school building, the doors and windows are all open and I can put you on the easel right by the door if you are more comfortable," Burgess said as he started to walk towards the school building.

"Thank you," Lily said. She glanced briefly over her shoulder and gave me a little wave. I smiled and waved back at her before heading into the medical unit to find Larissa.

Chapter Thirty-Six

Nash

I could hear Lily chatting away as I came in through the front door, which put a huge smile on my lips. She had taken to Maddox immediately when she met him. He sat up with her of a night when she woke with a nightmare. She seemed to adore him, and I think the feeling was mutual.

"Papa," Lily cried causing me to stop dead in the doorway. She grinned up at me. I looked over her head to Maddox who nodded his head and gave me a wink. "Come see what I painted today."

Lily took my hand and dragged me into the hallway where a huge canvas hung on the wall. It was a colorful picture with five people in it.

"Who are the people, Lily?" I asked.

She grinned and started to point at the people. "That's me in the middle, that's you with the big beard." As I looked at the picture, I could see the resemblance. "That is Dad, and they are the babies."

My mouth opened and closed. Not only had she called me Papa, Maddox Dad but there were pictures of two little girls that were the babies. I turned to look at Maddox and then back at Lily.

Lily was smiling at me. "Do you like it, Papa?"

My mouth opened and closed again. "I love it, Lily, I'm just in a little bit of shock right now," I replied.

"About what?"

"Well for one, you called me Papa and Maddox Dad, which isn't a bad thing, it just took me by surprise," I said watching Lily's smile beam. It was the brightest I'd seen her smile so far. "And the other thing that has taken me by surprise is the fact that you've painted two babies."

Lily giggled. "Iver said that Dad was having two babies. Two girls. I was able to tell that they were unicorns."

I turned to look at Maddox who nodded his head. "We met Iver while we were out at the compound. He and Lily have become fast friends."

"That's awesome, Lily," I said.

Lily smiled and stepped towards me and circled her arms around my waist. "Nash?" she said looking up at me.

"Yeah, little one?"

"Can I keep calling you Papa?"

Tears burned in my eyes, and I swallowed hard. I nodded my head. "Of course, sweetheart," I said around the lump that had formed in my throat.

I wrapped my arms around Lily's shoulders and held her tight against my chest. "I love you, Papa," she whispered which was enough to do me in. My tears fell over my cheeks, and I pressed a kiss into the top of her head.

"I love you too, Lily pad," I said.

"I love you both too," Maddox said as he stepped into our hug.

A sob fell from my lips. "Fuck, how did I get so damned lucky," I cried.

"You deserve it, Daddy," Maddox said with a wink.

"Oh yeah, I forgot, Dad is a little. I don't think I'm a little, but I think I might be a middle," Lily announced.

I bit my cheek to stop the laugh that wanted to roll out of me. It wasn't necessarily that I found what she said was funny. It was just so unexpected.

"I will support you no matter what Lily," I replied.

"Thank you."

"Alright enough of these tears, Lily has been helping me to learn to cook. It turns out that Lily is an amazing chef. And I know that I can't even cook toast," Maddox said with a laugh.

"I thought something smelt delicious in here. What have you been cooking?" I asked.

"I found a recipe book that used to belong to your Mama, it was in my bag of belongings I was surprised that Stacey let me have it," Lily said with a shake of her head.

I chuckled and nodded my head. "I would say that Papa snuck it in. Maybe that was his little stick it to Stacey."

Lily shrugged her shoulders. "Maybe," she said with a sigh. "Anyway, I made her lasagna recipe."

I chuckled and glanced at Maddox who grinned. "The first meal that Nash ever brought me was lasagna."

"That very same lasagna," I said.

Lily gasped and grinned. "I hope I did it just as good."

"Well, it smells the same, so I reckon it should be perfect."

"And it should be ready, so will we sit and eat. Lily let me cut up the vegetables for the salad," Maddox laughed.

I chuckled and kissed the top of his head. "You did good baby boy."

Maddox winked up at me before pressing a quick kiss on my lips that told me that there was a promise of a very hot night instore for us.

Chapter Thirty-Seven

Maddox

"Are you ready, Maddox?" Dr. Osbourne asked.

I grinned. "I've been ready for weeks now," I laughed.

Dr. Osbourne chuckled. "I don't think your mate is overly ready," he whispered.

I glanced at the head of the bed where Nash stood. His cheeks were pale, and his eyes were wide. I admit that I might have been not very nice when I was in pain. But now I'd had an epidural and I could no longer feel the contractions that were overtaking my body. Nash still hadn't overcome the names I'd been calling him for getting me pregnant. I don't think we will be having any more children if Nash has his way.

Lily was sitting in the waiting room with Merza and Arcadia as they waited for our two little girls to arrive.

"Alright Maddox, I want you to give an almighty push," Dr. Osbourne said from between my legs. I grasped hold of Nash's hand and the nurse's hand on my other side and bore down with all my strength. The epidural made it impossible to feel anything, it was strange. I knew that the baby was moving through my birth canal, but I couldn't feel it.

"And breathe," Dr. Osbourne said. "I can see the first babe's hair. With the next push, we will have her head out."

I nodded my head and bore down once more. "Excellent Maddox," the nurse said.

"There is her head, one more push Maddox and we will have the first baby girl," Dr. Osbourne explained.

I gritted my teeth together and pushed hard. A loud shriek sounded through the room and Dr. Osbourne chuckled as he placed our first daughter on my chest. "Papa, would you like to cut the cord?"

Nash nodded and stepped down to cut the cord, but my focus was on the baby that was laid on my chest. Her face was screwed up in anger as she squawked at being pulled out of the comfort of my womb.

"Hey there beautiful girl," I whispered as I pressed a kiss to the top of her head. Her dark hair had a white stripe that ran through the middle. I stroked my fingers gently down over her back as I felt our bond slot into place.

"She's so beautiful," Nash gushed quietly. As soon as she heard his voice, her eyes roved to look up at him. Nash's eyes widened and he chuckled.

"She loves her Papa," I murmured, which made her move her eyes back to me.

"Have you decided on a name?" the nurse asked.

"Yes, this one will be Star," I replied.

"Lovely, well little Star, come with me, while I do some checks on her weight and size and Daddy births your sister, then I'll bring you back," the nurse said as she took Star out of my arms.

"Ready to meet your next little girl?" Dr. Osbourne asked.

I nodded my head. Nash took my hand again and I sucked in a deep breath as I bore down once more.

"Woah," Dr. Osbourne said with a chuckle. "She wants to come in fast."

One push and she was literally out. Another screech sounded through the room and my next daughter was placed on my chest. She was completely identical to her sister, right down to the same white stripe that ran through the middle of her dark hair.

"You sure know how to make gorgeous babies," the nurse said as she brought back Star wrapped in a pink blanket. "What are you naming Star's sister."

"Winter," I answered with a smile.

"That's the perfect name, I'll just do the checks and then I'll bring her right back."

I nodded my head and allowed her to take Winter from my chest. It didn't take long before I was cleaned up and being placed on a bed with clean sheets and holding my daughters in my arms.

"I'll go and get Lily, I think she is pretty desperate to meet her sisters," Nash chuckled.

I nodded. Lily was more excited about her sister's arrival than I was. She had orchestrated with March and Burgess to create a night scene in the girl's bedrooms. I'd crafted them cradles that looked like clouds. We had been so excited when I felt the first contractions begin.

"Daddy," Lily said with a broad grin.

"Hey Lily pad, wanna come meet your sisters," I said with a smile.

Lily nodded her head rapidly as she stepped up to the bed beside me. "This is Star, and this is Winter," I introduced.

"They are exactly the same, but I can see one tiny difference," Lily said.

"What is the difference?"

"Star has one blue eye and one green eye."

I looked closely and Lily was right. It wasn't completely noticeable, but her right eye was most definitely more green than blue. Almost aqua in color.

"Well, that will make it easy to tell them apart," I said with a laugh.

Lily nodded her head. "Would you like to cuddle with them?" Nash asked as he came into the room.

"Yes please."

"Come and sit on the couch and I'll bring them over to you," Nash directed.

Lily sat on the couch and Nash took Star out of my arms and laid her in Lily's arms followed by Winter. Lily leaned forward and pressed a tiny kiss on each of their heads before whispering something to them that I couldn't hear. When she looked up again, she had tears in her eyes.

"I'm always going to protect them," she declared.

"I believe you," I said. "You are going to be a wonderful big sister."

N ash

"Sorry to call you in off your parental leave early," Kade said as I came into the shifter unit room. I'd been off work for two weeks with the girls, I was supposed to have another two weeks, but Kade had rang early that morning and asked if I would be able to come in early.

I shook my head. "No stress. I figured something must have happened."

Kade nodded his head and turned to everyone that was in the room. "Alright, thank you everyone for coming. I'm sorry again for calling you all so early. I got a message from Rison this morning."

I knew this wasn't going to be good. Rison had gone back to the underworld to keep an eye on Ettore. It had been quiet for months. Ettore hadn't left the underworld and we had been able to concentrate on finding other kids that had been taken over the years.

"Ettore left the underworld last night, with Brooklyn and the baby," Kade said.

"Shit," Memphis growled. "Do we know where he went?"

Kade sighed and nodded his head. "Yeah. He dropped Brooklyn off at the Devil's Advocates compound and then disappeared with the child."

"Oh no," Coltrane moaned.

"So, I'm assuming he hasn't gone back to the underworld with the kid?" I asked.

Kade nodded. "Yeah, he hasn't returned."

"The house that he has here on earth?" Merza asked.

"Scout and Nova are watching it with Jabari and Hawke, but at this stage, they haven't been able to sense him there. It is possible that he has other homes all over the world and could be anywhere, but what we do know is that he is on earth and has the baby with him," Kade replied.

"And Brooklyn is she alright?" I asked.

"No," Bacchus answered. "She was found just clinging to life at the guardhouse when they did a changeover."

"He beat her?" Memphis asked.

"No. She looks like she has been poisoned but we can't work out with what. Arcadia is out there now with Kaki and Oakland as they try to find what it is that she has in her. But we can't be sure that she is going to survive," Bacchus replied.

"Shit," I growled.

Suddenly Scout came rushing into the room. "We've found him."

"Where?" Kade growled.

"He's just shown up at the old Morpheus training facility, but it's not good."

"What is it?" Kade asked.

"He has over three hundred alphas with him."

I gasped and my eyes widened. "From the underworld?"

"No, bred."

"Where the hell did, he get them from?" Merza asked.

"I don't know, but once again we are on the fucking back foot," Kade growled as he slammed his fist into the table in front of him.

"Is he planning to restart Morpheus?" I questioned.

"I don't know," Scout replied with a shake of their head. "Whatever he is planning on doing with the alphas can't be good. No unmated omega is now safe."

I thought about Lily and my heart clenched. "How are we going to stop this?"

"There is only one way to stop this and that's to kill him," Bacchus spat.

"How? Every time we've tried, he has evaded us," I argued.

"We will end him," Kade growled. His eyes were glowing the deepest red I'd ever seen. "I will fucking end him."

The end.

Don't miss out!

Visit the website below and you can sign up to receive emails whenever S L Davies publishes a new book. There's no charge and no obligation.

https://books2read.com/r/B-A-NZRR-HQDBC

BOOKS 2 READ

Connecting independent readers to independent writers.

Also by S L Davies

Breeding Facility
Memphis
Bacchus
Coltrane
Pax
Raiden
Nash

Devil's Advocates
Lynx
Israel

KINK
Freya
Tanquil

Onyx Rebels
Onyx Rebels Prologue

Standalone
Sisters Revenge
Killer Love
Soldiers At War
Second Chances

About the Author

S L Davies is an Australian Author living in Country, Victoria. She is inspired by the world around her.

Read more at https://www.amazon.com/~/e/B0832T8F7Z.